Harry Potter Fans Rejoice!

Here is a new novel which offers us a rare glimpse into the ancient world of Cherokee wizards. Set in a timeless aboriginal past, *The First Raven Mocker* is a coming of age story which follows a young Indian boy's quest to learn the fine art of black magic. Along the way, he encounters witches, sorcerers, and man-eating giants. However, as the reader soon learns, this is the archetypal Hero's journey with a twist.

Courtney Miller has created an imaginative adventure tale, one which captures the ethos of Cherokee folklore and myth.

—Alan Kilpatrick, Professor
American Indian Studies
San Diego State University and
author of *The Night Has a Naked Soul*

The First Raven Mocker

Courtney Miller

Popul Vuh
Publishing

Cover Design: Nick Zelinger, NZ Graphics
Interior Design: Ronnie Moore, WESType Publishing Services, Inc.
Editing: John Maling, Editing by John
Book Consultant: Judith Briles, The Book Shepherd
Published by: Popul Vuh Publishing
               PO Box 91
               Westcliffe, CO 81252
Printer: Color House Graphics

ISBN: 978-0-9887711-0-9 (paperback)
ISBN: 978-0-9887711-1-6 (e-Pub)

Library of Congress Control Number: 2013910851

1. Native American—Fiction   2. Cherokee—Fiction
3. Immortalism—Fiction   4. Witchcraft—Fiction   5. Cultural
Heritage—Fiction   6. Mythology—Fiction   7. Sagas—Fiction

First Edition   Printed in USA

For Elsie Bass Guthrie

*The teacher who believed in me and
inspired me to write.*

Acknowledgments

No book comes together without the help of many dedicated people. I would like to acknowledge Elsie Bass Guthrie, my High School English teacher whose dedication was an inspiration and whose encouragement gave me the confidence to try. My wife, Lin's, support was vital. Dr. Judith Briles' encyclopedic knowledge of the industry and selfless dedication to making authors successful has been essential for putting the book together and understanding the business side of writing. I'd like to thank John Maling for his insightful editing; Nick Zelinger for the beautiful cover; Ronnie Moore for the creative layout of the book; and Deb Courtney and Mary Karen Meredith for their perspicacious critiques.

I would like to acknowledge the author James Mooney, whose years spent interviewing the Cherokee and resulting book *Myths of the Cherokee and Sacred Formulas of the Cherokees* preserved the richness and beauty of the ancient Cherokee culture of antiquity; the old Cherokee Medicine man, Swimmer, and Frans M. Olbrechts whose manuscript preserved the Cherokee sacred formulas and medical prescriptions; Alan Kilpatrick whose wonderful book, *The Night Has a Naked Soul* helped me understand the concept of the four askinas and Cherokee witchcraft; and the great drawings and concise presentation of the Cherokee culture by Thomas A. Mails so helpful in picturing the people and places. Many thanks to Nachez principal chief, Hutke Fields, for helping with the character names.

Misconceptions—
The Real Cherokee

THE CHEROKEE CHRONICLES WAS born out of the research I have done over the years on Native American cultures. I discovered that what I thought I knew about Native Americans was based on the Hollywood fixation on the Plains Indians and the stereotypical "noble savage." In an introduction to the book *Incidents of Travel in Yucatan*, Victor Wolfgang von Hagen wrote, "The acceptance of an indigenous 'civilization' demanded of an American living in 1836 a complete reorientation; to him an 'Indian' was one of those barbaric, half-naked tipi dwellers, a rude sub-human people who hunted with animal stealth."

The Cherokee were nothing like the savage, nomadic, hunter-gatherers portrayed in movies and TV. The Cherokee never lived in tipis; they have never worn feathered head-dresses (except maybe to please tourists); they didn't ride horses until the Europeans brought them over; there were no Cherokee princesses; they didn't follow the buffalo around; the "squaw" didn't humbly follow ten paces behind her husband; they didn't worship a panoply of gods; they weren't, by any definition of the word, savages.

When describing them in the *Ascent of Man*, author and philosopher Jacob Bronowski observed, "The largest step in the ascent of man is the change from nomad to village agriculture." Long before the Europeans came to

America, the Cherokee had made that giant leap and were an agriculturally-based culture that built permanent, framed, mud stucco houses in well-organized villages secured by palisaded walls. They had sophisticated social structures and highly developed government. Each village was governed by a peace chief and a war chief. During peace times, a white flag flew over the majestic, seven-sided council house and the peace chief ruled. In times of war, a red flag flew over the council house and the war chief ruled. Villagers were organized by families or clans. Each clan had its purpose and responsibilities within the tribe and its members were governed and lived by the rules of each clan. Each of the seven clans preserved and taught one of the seven tenants that enabled the pure to ascend through the seven levels of personal development.

The Cherokee were a matriarchal society. The children were born into the clan of their mother and were raised by the tenants of her clan. The women owned the houses and fields. The highest ranking women were known as the "Beloved Women" and were responsible for divining justice. Women could marry and divorce as they pleased. When a man proposed, he brought a deer to her doorstep. She would confide in her grandmother for advice. If she decided to accept marriage, she simply brought in the deer and prepared an acceptance feast. A divorce was simple. The woman simply placed her husband's belongings outside the house on the doorstep. When he came home, he got the message.

If a clan member committed a crime, it was up to his clan to administer justice. The punishment for murder might require his family to bind his hands and feet and push him off a cliff to his death on the rocks below.

There were no Kings (and consequently no Princesses). The Cherokee Government at both the local level and at the national level was bicameral—a "white" organization that governed over the peace and "red" organization that governed over war. The person of highest authority in the white branch was the High Priest, known as the "Uku". Below him were assistants and priests from each clan and they were responsible for administering civil law, invoking blessings and prayers for religious well-being, removing the uncleanness from polluted persons to restore them to physical well-being, and they planned and supervised the important ceremonies and celebrations throughout the year.

The red branch of government was made up of a complimentary set of officials whose responsibilities were exclusively related to war. Author Thomas E. Mails explained, "If either of the two organizations was in any way subordinate to the other, it was the red group, since the Great High Priest could make or unmake the war chiefs. In addition, the red officials were at frequent intervals elected by popular vote, while the white officials were either to some extent hereditary or subject to appointment by the Great High Priest. ... In most instances, red officials acquired their rank as the result of bravery in battle ..."

Mails goes on to say, "An assemblage of Beloved Women ... was present at every war council. These served as counselors to the male leaders, and also regulated the treatment dealt to prisoners of war."

The Cherokee maintained a well-organized military. The Wolf Clan was primarily responsible for providing warriors, therefore, children of the wolf clan were trained in warfare from the time they could walk. Many games were created to help develop children's skills. And some games became as prominent and important to the village and the nation as football, baseball, or soccer is to us today. It is said that sometimes war between tribes was avoided by settling the dispute through an Anetsa (Ball Play game similar to La Crosse).

The Cherokee definitely don't fit the stereotypes we attribute to Native Americans. They deserve to be remembered as a civilized nation. I have tried in this book and subsequent books in the Cherokee Chronicles to portray the Cherokee as they really were. I want to tell their story through the fictional eyes of a representative family starting around 1,000 A.D. and end the series with those courageous families that witnessed the end of their traditional culture and struggled to build new lives."

Characters

Ugidahli Unega (Ugi), [oo-gee-dah-lee oo-nay-guh
(oo-gee)]
"White Feather"—young boy (main character),
Deer Clan
Kalanu Ahkyeliski, [cah-lah-noo awk-yee-lee-ss-kee]
"Raven Mocker"—the first of this kind of witch
Nunyunuwi, [noon-you-new-wee]
"Stone Clad"—cannibal witch who wears a suit of
stones
Nvwoti Atlisdodi Usdi, [new-woh-tee aht-lees-doh-
dee oos-dee]
"Little Medicine Bowl"—a Yunwi Tsunsdi
[yoon-wee choons-dee], "Little People"
Awi Ganvnvi, [ah-wee gah-new-new-ee]
"Dear Track"—Ugi's mother, Deer Clan
Yona Utana, [yoh-nah oo-tah-nah]
"Great Bear"—Ugi's father, Bear Clan
Awi-e Usdi, [ah-wee-ee oo-ss-dee]
"Little Elk"—Ugi's maternal uncle, Deer Clan
Awinita Uloge, [ah-wee-nee-tah oo-low-gee]
"Crazy Fawn"—Ugi's maternal aunt, Deer Clan
Tlvdatsi Sakonige, [tloo-dah-chee sah-koh-nee-gee]
"Blue Panther"—Ugi's girlfriend, Long Hair clan
Galonedv Adutlvdodi (Adawehi), [gah-low-nee-dew
ah-doot-lew-doh-dee (Ah-dah-way-hee]
"Painted Mask(Wizard)"—Ugi's mentor, old
witch/wizard, Paint Clan

Yona Gunuge "Ajilvsgi", [yoh-nah goo-noo-gee
"ah-gee-lews-gee"]
"Black Bear (Flower)"—old woman witch, Bear Clan
Yona Aji, [yoh-nah ah-gee]
"Bear Mother"—Ugi's paternal grandmother,
Bear Clan
Yona Hahesosta (Udo), [yoh-nah ha-hee-sos-tah
(oo-doh)]
"Bear Dreamer (Brother)"—Ugi's paternal uncle,
Bear Clan
Yona Ulvnotisgi Ugowe, [yoh-nah oo-lew-noh-tees-
gee oo-goh-wee]
"Crazy Bear Leader"—Ugi's paternal uncle,
Bear Clan
Yona Ahuli, [yoh-nah ah-who-lee]
"Drumming Bear"—Ugi's paternal uncle,
Bear Clan
Sali, [saw-lee]
"Persimmon Bark"—young Clan Elder,
Wild Potato Clan

The four souls of the victim reside in his saliva, blood, bile, and bone marrow. By consuming them, whatever life the victim would have had now belongs to the Raven Mocker.

THE OLD CHEROKEE UKU sat at the edge of the precipice high above his village as daylight waned and darkness approached. Sister Sun relaxed as she ended her long journey across the sky vault and breathed a cooling sigh sweeping away the sweltering heat. It was not the darkness of night that disturbed him, but the dark world of witchcraft now confronting him. Adanvdo Alsgia, "Dances with Spirits" closed the gap on his white, feathery cape and ignored the tickle on his nose as the feathers danced in the chilling breeze. He listened closely to the footsteps shuffling across the well-worn, rocky path. The intruder paused quietly behind him saying nothing but audibly breathing heavily. The old Uku could sense the nervousness and dread of his visitor. "Come sit with me, Grandson. Tell me what troubles your heart."

The young apprentice approached and awkwardly lowered his tall, lanky body to sit beside his great grandfather. Rocking noisily back and forth, he pulled his heavy bear cape out from under him enough to enshroud himself. The old man waited patiently for him to get comfortable. He knew the question the young man had come to ask; the question he had dreaded answering; the question that could change everything.

Young Ahyeli-a had been the ideal student all his life. He had earned his name "Mimic" as a child because of his amazing memory and ability to repeat verbatim the stories told him by his grandmother. He had tagged along with his great grandfather faithfully absorbing all that the wise old Uku could teach him about medicine, conjures, connecting with the spirits, restoring balance and harmony to those who had faltered or had the "thing put under them" and needed help returning to wellness.

Ahyeli-a had mastered the white way and in time would become a wise healer and perhaps even replace his great grandfather as Uku, the highest position a medicine man and priest can achieve in his village. But, his training would not be complete until he also mastered the dark ways. To defeat witchcraft, the Uku must know the dark ways as well as the witch. But the dark ways had tempted and turned many attracted to the allure of its magic. This was what Adanvdo feared.

"Who is Kalanu Akyeliski? Why is he called Raven Mocker?"

The Uku shifted uncomfortably, "Tsigili." he whispered, spitting out the word in disgust. He wanted there to be no doubt that a "witch" was something to be despised.

Ahyeli-a frowned and studied the old Uku as he waited for the explanation. His teacher took a deep breath to control his hatred before starting his curious apprentice down that dark path of knowledge.

"He doesn't MOCK the raven, he BECOMES the raven."

Adanvdo shifted and pulled his cape even closer, using the cape subconsciously more for security than for warmth. He anticipated the question his great grandson dared not interrupt him to ask. "You will be able to distinguish him from a common raven. When he flies, his wings and tail blaze, leaving a trail of sparks."

A fiery meteorite streaked across the sky catching the attention of the two, on edge because of the troublesome subject. Ahyeli-a looked questioningly at his mentor. The mentor's gaze remained on the spot where the streaking, fiery stone had flamed out. He didn't believe in coincidences and he had taught that lesson to his apprentice. But, he wasn't sure himself what the meaning of this occurrence was. Was it significant? A sign? It was in any case awkward timing. He decided to store the event in the back of his mind and consider its significance later.

For Ahyeli-a's benefit, Adanvdo shook his head dismissing the event, refocused on the fading mountain peaks in the distance and then continued the lesson in a whisper. "The Raven Mocker seeks out the weak or frail and enters their house unseen to torment them—to literally scare them to death. Invisible, he may shake their bed, pull things from the wall, or even pick up his victim and hurl them to the floor. He may shape-shift into a ferocious panther or horrifying bear. Then, at that critical moment of death, he sucks their dying breath from them as he plunges his fist into their chest to extract their heart, liver and rib bone."

Remembering the look on his great grandson's face when they examined the Raven Mocker's latest victim, he was compelled to explain, "Afterwards, no trace of the entry is visible on the chest of the victim."

He anticipated his clever student's next question ... "The four souls of the victim reside in his saliva, blood, bile, and bone marrow. By consuming them, whatever life the victim would have had now belongs to the Raven Mocker."

On a rocky crag cut into the face of a sheer cliff, Kalanu Akyeliski, the Raven Mocker, sat beside a sterile pond staring into the water-covered crystal shimmering in his bluish, diseased hand. Within could be seen images of the two men perched high over the precipice. Sadly, he placed his dripping crystal back into the netted pouch of his necklace. "Is that what I am, Adanvdo?"

How had his life come to this? He had never intended to become the most dreaded and hated tsigili ever to walk the face of the earth. Sadly, the lonely, decrepit old witch pushed himself up and pulled his tattered, black, raven-feathered cape tightly around his chilled, withering, fragile body and limped into his small, seven-sided hut.

He stoked the smoldering embers in his hearth until they glowed red and ignited. He laid a handful of twigs on the fragile flames followed by a small log. He had dealt with loneliness all his life. His proud, stoic father had been a loner who spent little time with him. His flighty, self-centered mother had treated him as a nuisance and a pest. Living deep in the woods and far from any village or other family, he had been forced to find solace alone in the forest.

His mind drifted back to his thirteenth summer. A time before his journey down the dark path, before his name was Raven Mocker, when he was known as Ugidahli Unega, "White Feather". The summer when his father had failed to return one night from a hunting trip, and his mother had, against his objections, taken him forceably into the village to stay with his mother's family while his uncle led the search to find his father. He had despised the village with its precocious residents and complex social customs. Then the decrepit old witch smiled at a memory. "That's when I first saw her."

He gasped in horror at the fleshless face with empty eye sockets staring back at him.

SHE WAS, IN HER every movement, the most fascinating thing Ugidahli Unega had ever seen. She captured his complete attention. Hiding behind a Blue Holly bush, he studied her every detail, the way she carried her basket in the crook of her arm as if it were contaminated and she loathed it touching her; the way she picked each strawberry and examined it before placing it in the basket or taking a bite. The way she closed her eyes and bit into the tip of the strawberry enclosing it with her lips and sucking to make sure no juices spilled off; the way she enjoyed its taste as she slowly chewed the crunchy, luscious fruit. Nothing on earth compared to her beauty and her appeal.

As the lithesome beauty strolled to the next strawberry bush, her skirt swaying with each step as she pushed her long, shiny black hair back from her face, her beautiful, dark, round eyes stared into the sky at nothing in particular. As she moved to his left, leaning to keep her in his view, he lost his balance and fell into the bush where he was hiding. Repositioning himself, he kept watching her to see if she had seen or heard him. She stopped chewing only momentarily before continuing on as if she had not heard him. He thought he detected a slight, fleeting smile on her perfect lips before she disappeared into the forest.

Love-struck, he rocked back, embraced his legs, rested his chin on his knees, and sat dreaming of this wondrous creature. Images of her fleeting smile; her swaying hips; her lips embracing the luscious fruit flashed through his mind. Fire stirred in his stomach and desire filled him. His solitary life in the forest, away from village life, had not prepared him for this.

Distant voices interrupted his fantasy. Something was happening. Maybe the search party had returned with his father. The anxious boy leaped to his feet and raced toward the village, zigzagging through the thick forest up the incline over the crest and down the slope, reaching the edge of the bluff overlooking it. He looked down on the villagers pouring into the valley from the fortress-like compound. The focus of the crowd was on the small search party carrying a body in a make-shift stretcher.

"Father?" he whispered.

He raced down the grassy slope to join the onlookers but he stumbled, fell and rolled down into the unsuspecting crowd. When they saw it was Ugidahli Unega, they respectfully parted allowing him through. They knew the recovered body was his father. He gasped in horror at the hideous sight on the stretcher. A fleshless face with empty eye sockets stared back at him and the bloody, shredded chest cavity of the corpse, was now devoid of organs. *Who is this? Where's my father?*

Opposite the search team, his mother's scream was heard. Her brothers were holding her on either side as her head flopped back and her body went limp. "Yona Utana ... Yona Utana ..." She chanted her husband's name over and over.

He was confused. *Where was his father? What happened to the poor person on the carrier?* He stood shocked as the procession passed him. Ugidahli ran to his uncle, Awi-e Usdi. "Where's Father? Didn't you find Father?"

Turning, he glared at his nephew and placed his hand on the boy's shoulder. With lips trembling, his eyes turned to the dead man on the carrier. "Ugi, that IS your father."

Ugi looked at the mutilated corpse on the carrier. That was not his father. Why did they think this skinny remnant was Yona Utana—the "Great Bear." His father was a huge man.

The crowd hushed and moved back to make room for three elders and a younger man with a round, baby face, puffy cheeks and dark, beady eyes. The four men huddled around the carrier to study the body. One elder turned to Awi-e Usdi. "What has happened here?"

Awi-e Usdi, in his most authoritative manner, said, "We found him beside the carcass of the deer he had slain. He must have been carrying it home on his shoulders at night, prompting the night predators to attack."

The inquiring elder nodded gratefully to Awi-e Usdi and looked back sadly at the corpse. Ugidahli Unega wanted to protest. Couldn't they see that this was not his father?

The younger man whispered, "Cannibal."

The elders waved the procession on. The stunned boy stood immobile as the crowd filed in through the palisaded village entrance. Their murmurs subsided as the last of the procession disappeared into the compound, leaving thick clouds of dust to rise and spread. Gritty dirt peppered his sweaty face and filled his nose. He opened his mouth and licked the salty powder from his lips as the cloud began to disperse. Amazed, he observed a white, ghost-like apparition slowly appear in the midst of the vanishing cloud. Ugidahli Unega's heart began to pump and consciousness flooded back into his brain.

There she was again. The girl from the strawberry patch was standing there, with her weight shifted to one side and one leg slack, the basket of strawberries dangling below one extended arm, the other crooked with her hand holding back her long, black hair dancing around her face in the swirling dust driven by the wind. Her dark, impassionate eyes studied the devastated boy.

The power of the moment overwhelmed him; he began to tremble, and tears gushed from his eyes. He dropped his head into his hands to hide his weakness. Then, quickly wiping his face and getting hold of himself, he took a deep breath, straightened up and bravely looked back to find only a dirt devil swirling where the girl had once stood.

Ugidahli Unega dropped to his knees and wept again.

*The plants and the animals
were friends of sorts in that
they never chastised him
the way his mother did.
But they never consoled him
nor offered advice the way
the tiny little man did.*

THE SHADE FROM THE overhanging tree and the spray from the babbling stream was a cool relief from the heat of the day. Sister Sun was now heading down the sky vault on the last half of her journey. Seeking answers from the stream and the whispering pines, Ugidahli Unega sat on a wet boulder listening patiently. The no-nonsense attitude of the rushing water passed him with no concern for his crisis. The breeze blowing through the cottonwoods making the leaves clatter, usually reminded him of rain falling, but this morning they were laughing at him. Even the vibrant flowers looked dull and held back the sweet perfume in preference for the pungent odor of mud and dead grass.

"He IS dead, you know."

Ugidahli jerked around. It was his little friend the Yunwi Tsunsdi. The plants and the animals were friends of sorts in that they never chastised him the way his mother did. But they never consoled him nor offered advice the way the tiny little man did. His grandmother had once warned him not to speak of the Yunwi Tsunsdi.

She explained that they were very private people who lived in the caves high in the mountains where they spent their days singing and dancing and playing tricks on wayward travelers who unwittingly ventured too close. She told him that the Yunwi Tsunsdi could make themselves invisible if they wanted and usually only appeared to little children who needed their help.

It had been many summers since he had been visited by his little friend and had assumed that he had grown too old to be helped anymore.

"But Father was too powerful to be defeated by a panther. He killed panthers and bears."

The gust rattled the trees violently bending the branches to block the boy's view of the Yunwi Tsunsdi. Did the little wizard answer? Had he angered him?

As the breeze faded and the branches danced back to their relaxed position, only gray hair remained draped across the stair-stepped stones where he had been sitting. The desperate boy rubbed his eyes in hopes that they were deceiving him, but only the gray strands of mossy hair lay before him. The dwarf had always told him the truth, even when it was not what he wanted to hear. But this time his little friend was wrong.

Sullen and defeated, he trudged slowly back to his aunt's house. It was a rectangular, gabled, frame house, coated with smooth, fresh mud plaster. The cypress bark shingles still smelled sweet on the newly built house. As he entered the main room through the front door, his mother's wails echoed through the shadowy, sparsely decorated room. Her shadow danced on the walls as she rocked back and forth beside the unattended embers slowly burning down in the hearth. A sweet, fruity smell like carrot mixed with a sour, rotten odor attacked his nostrils. He traced the smells to the corpse of his father lying on a wood bench against the back wall where his aunt, his mother's sister, Awinita, was busy cleaning the body with a mixture of water and willow root. The smell was overpowering.

Could that frail remains really be his father? He tried to imagine his father's face on the bare frame of the skull. The shoulders were broad but the decimated chest and stomach were too shallow. Then he saw it. The handle of his father's distinctive knife sheathed and strapped to his side. The chill in his chest left him numb and anxious.

He slipped back out of the house. He rubbed the nape of his neck as a warm breeze lifted his hair slightly and tickled his sweaty neck. His aunt stepped out behind him. "Don't go far, Ugi, we must go to your house and pull all of your father's things out tonight."

Ugi shivered and began to tremble, "Why?"

"All of his possessions are defiled now."

His lower lip stiffened, "Why?"

The soft-hearted aunt, only a few years his senior stepped up to hug her troubled nephew. "Oh, Ugi, I know it is hard, but your father is gone now. You must release his spirit so it can find its way to the upper world."

Ugi pulled away and turned to his aunt, "Where is my father? Who is that in there?"

His startled aunt teared up. Her soft, round face wrinkled as she hugged herself tightly, "Ugi. That IS your father in there. Didn't they tell you?"

"That's not Father. Father was a giant."

His aunt shivered; she was aghast at her nephew's denial. She hesitated before responding. "Come back in, Ugi, and comfort your mother. She needs you right now."

He didn't want to comfort his mother. He wanted to flee from these ignorant people who couldn't, for some strange reason, see that the man on the bench was not his father.

Tears streamed from his eyes as he clenched his fists and held his stiff arms close to his sides. His aunt grimaced and then pleaded, "Come in Ugi. Uncle Awi-e will be here soon, and he can explain these things to you."

"No." Ugi retorted, "I don't want him to explain things to me … I want my Father."

Finally collapsing into his aunt's arms, she cradled him, sharing his grief and pain with tears of sympathy.

Resigned to his fate, Ugi sat outside the house, immune to the incessant wailing of his mother inside. Miraculously, her crying ceased when Awi-e Usdi entered the house. Neither Ugi nor his aunt mentioned Ugi's outburst. Instead, the family collected themselves and silently began the long walk to the house of his father, now vacant.

Ugi caught a glimpse of the Yunwi Tsunsdi leaning up against a tree with arms folded and a challenging look on his face. Ugi looked away in shame. He knew in his heart that everyone was right after all, and his father would not be returning—ever.

He stared into the dark sky at the thousands of spirit campfires. The smoky streak of "maize" littering the sky dome reminded him of a time long ago when he sat with his father on a boulder next to the stream that flowed past their old house and listened to the story of the naughty spirit wolf that raided the maize bin and then tracked it across the sky. He tried to understand why there were not more moments like that with his father.

What had he done to push his father away? He dropped his head; his father had never pushed him away, he just had never pulled his son in. His father was not like his mother who verbalized her every thought. Instead, his father had been a quiet man who rarely spoke. Ugi had been both afraid and in awe of his huge, silent father. The gentle man had never given him reason to be afraid, not really, but his solemn father had never been loving, nor reached out to him either. Ugi's heart ached for his father and he longed to crawl into his father's lap one more time.

Moonlight illuminated the familiar lines of the vacant house, once Ugi's home, as they approached. The old, rotting shingles glistened on one side and were shadowy blue on the other. The mud plaster sides reflected white on the moon side but were black on the porch side. Returning like this made the house cold and frightening. It smelled musty and pungent. Not the warm, inviting smells of bread and corn cooking. The smells of life—sweat, tanned leather, feathers—were replaced with smells of death—brittle, dried leather, rotting wood, and dead mice. The light from uncle's blazing torch cast a glowing circle around his uncle as he stepped under the porch roof. He waited for the rest of the party to step into the light ring and then handed the torch to his older sister, Ugi's mother. She calmly took the lead.

"His tools and utensils will be buried with him, so pile them next to the hearth. Everything else of his we can pile out here," she said.

There was no sign of the debilitating grief that his mother had been exhibiting since his father's corpse had been returned. She was calm and resolute and fell with ease into the familiar role of matriarch around her brothers and sister. No one spoke as they went about the house gathering up Yona Utana's possessions.

Ugi stood alone inside the doorway and watched the impassionate operation. His heart stung as his father's old bow, stone hatchet, bear-skin cape and rabbit-fur pouches were unceremoniously removed from the wall and tossed beside the hearth. He stepped to one side as his uncles passed with his father's bunk. In only a few moments, they were done. His mother stood solemnly beside the hearth clutching her chin with her thumb and forefinger as her siblings stood respectfully about her awaiting her command.

"Ok, that's it." She reported with finality. Her younger sister hugged her from the side gently and then they all turned and marched out of the house. Ugi stared at his father's scant tools and utensils clumped on the floor next to the hearth as the glow from the torch subsided leaving the room totally dark. *Is that it? Is that all there is to a man's life?* He lamented. Something didn't feel right. Something was missing. *How could this man who had been so important to this family now be just an insignificant pile of tools?*

The flesh was sliced neatly as with a knife. The face was cut and peeled neatly off the skull; the work of a cannibal.

THE TALL, VERTICAL POLES that formed the palisaded walls of the village formed a dark and jagged silhouette against an orange, smoky glow from inside. Nearing the village walls, they could hear the drums pounding from the dance grounds where many danced around the huge fire to mourn his father's death. Ugi paused unnoticed inside the entrance as his family strode purposefully toward their house. Drawn to the congregation surrounding the dancers and the fire, he found himself standing behind the elders.

They were enjoying their ceremonial pipes stuffed with their individual blends of sacred tobacco. Although he was focused on the lavishly costumed dancers, he overheard the name uttered by the odd young man sitting with the elders: "Nunyunuwi."

"Stone Clad"? The monster his mother had threatened would eat him when he wanted to stay out past dark? Another elder removed his pipe to speak. "Didn't the search party say a panther was drawn to him by the bloody deer carcass he carried on his shoulders?"

The young man persisted, "The flesh was not ripped from his bones, it was cut. Stone Clad is a cannibal. The hunter ventured too far to hunt for his deer."

The three elders and their younger associate resumed smoking thoughtfully. Ugidahli Unega was confused. According to his mother, the evil giant wore stones over his body to deflect arrows and war club strikes; he sometimes raided villages to carry off women or children and kill the men. She told him that she had heard stories of hunters who ventured deep into unfamiliar territory and were killed and eaten by that wretched cannibal.

One of the elders spoke, "Why would Nunyunuwi not eat the deer instead?"

"Nunyunuwi does not fancy the meat of the deer, only the meat of the hunter."

An elder added, "The deer WAS eaten. Awi-e Usdi said the deer had been ripped open and its entrails missing."

"The victim of predators. The cannibal would have dressed out the deer."

Another elder enjoined, "Sali is right. The flesh was sliced neatly as with a knife. The face was cut and peeled neatly off the skull; the work of a cannibal."

Tears filled Ugidahli's eyes and fear filled his stomach. He ran into the darkness, away from the fire and the elders. It could not be true. He could not accept that his father had been eaten by a cannibal. His giant father could defeat anyone. No one was as strong as the man aptly named "the Great Bear"—no one was as fierce.

The traumatized boy stumbled through the village entrance and wandered blindly into the forest. He found himself standing at the edge of a clearing opening up to a crystal pond below a waterfall. The heat of the day vanished here with the cool breeze blowing across the spray of the waterfall. The sweet smell of the fresh water and lush vegetation drew him.

A night hawk screeched its tri-note shrill. Ugidahli Unega glanced up just as the nocturnal hunter glided across the full moon and trilled again. He saw that there were two of them. His gaze returned to the peaceful waterfall glistening in the moonlight. The shimmering reflection of the moon formed a path from the waterfall across the pond to him inviting him to follow it into the underworld.

Something moved in the wake of the moonlit path. The startled boy's eyes adjusted to the darkness and focused on the shadowy nude figure standing with the frigid waters encircling her thighs dimpled with gooseflesh and glistening in the moonlight. With water dripping and running down her arm, she raised her cupped hands to the sky making an offering to the spirits of the west. She squatted and plunged her head into the water. As she stood again, the pond seemed to rise up with her and then drain away revealing her bulging breasts and supple nipples briefly before being covered by her bent arms. The silvery chimera palmed the water from her eyes and face as she turned away from her audience to make her offering to the north.

Ugidahli Unega shivered and, smitten, felt the pang of anxiety in his loins. The infatuated boy crept over to sit on a flat boulder beside the pond. Clumsily, he stepped on a rotting branch which snapped loudly beneath his foot. He froze. The interrupted enchantress twisted to look behind her clasping her hands between her breasts. Ugidahli Unega held his breath hoping that his shadow would blend with the dark forest behind him. The alerted bather cocked her head to one side as if studying the shadows. The ogling boy's heart raced. Her eyes searched all along the pond's edge, then resumed her north facing position and raked her fingers up through her soaked hair turning her face upward into the moon. Ugidahli Unega's lungs betrayed him; he gasped deeply for air.

The girl withdrew her fingers from her hair slowly and without turning, calmly, almost musically, inquired, "Who is there?"

Ugidahli Unega swallowed hard.

"Speak! Who are you?"

He instinctively backed away. His discoverer turned and raked her wet, stringy hair from her face as she pushed through the water to the bank toward the shivering boy. The discovered spy scrambled backward, and stumbling, turned and fled.

As the despondent boy neared his house, the mournful wails of his mother grew louder. He slapped his hands over his ears and grimaced. He could not bear to listen to her cries that night.

Sheepishly, he entered the small, rectangular, main room of the house. His mother sat beside the hearth cradled by her sister. Her brothers sat stoically around the circle of stones that contained the low, simmering fire.

Curiously, they were wearing ragged clothing, and ashes could be seen glistening from their head and shoulders. No one noticed him. He quietly stepped back out of the house. He didn't know where he would go, but he knew that he could not stay there tonight.

He wrapped his arms around himself and let his tears flow. He dropped to his knees, bent over and pressed his forehead against the ground. Tonight he would cry himself to sleep.

Looking back, Ugidahli Unega remembered that the last time he saw his father alive, his father was as happy as he could be which, he thought regretfully, was still pretty grim. It was, he now knew, because his father loved to hunt and was anticipating the hunt he had planned for the next day—his last hunt. His father had been a quiet man who stayed to himself. He was large and powerful and no one ever challenged him that Ugidahli Unega could remember—except his mother.

Yona Utana had slipped out of the house that fateful morning while his wife and son slept. It is unlikely that either one even thought about him that day until the darkness of the evening reminded them that he had not returned. Ugidahli Unega remembered his mother waiting up by the hearth through the night and found her gazing out the door when he awoke the next morning.

When his father did not return the next morning, she had gone to her brother, Awi-e Usdi, who put together a search party. She had gone through the motions of doing her daily chores, but Ugidahli Unega knew, even at his young age, that his mother's mind was on her husband's absence. The search party had returned that evening empty-handed. It would be four days later that his mangled body was discovered near the carcass of the deer he had slain. The hunters had naturally speculated that he had been attacked coming home by a panther while carrying the carcass over his shoulders in the dark.

The shock of seeing the corpse with its face torn off and the eyes missing from the bony sockets would haunt Ugidahli Unega for the rest of his life.

Ugidahli Unega did not share his father's love of hunting. But with the death of his father, it was now up to him to provide for his mother. And it was up to his uncle, his mother's brother, to teach him to hunt. He hated his uncle. He and his father did have that in common. But tradition dictated that a son must follow the customs of his mother's clan, not his father's. The Cherokee were a matriarchal society and the children belonged to the mother. A Cherokee did not go against clan law.

But even after thirteen summers, no matriarchal uncle had stepped forth to teach Ugidahli Unega the ways of his clan. His mother had seemed content to let him learn only the minimal customs from her. He remembered a bitter argument between his father and uncle. His father had been straddling the stream standing on two widely spaced stones with his spear cocked and ready for a passing fish when his uncle had stormed out to the bank and chastised his father for taking away his sister to live in the wilderness instead of living with the family, as tradition would dictate.

"The boy knows nothing of his clan nor how to hunt." His uncle complained.

His huge father had calmly continued to study the water with his spear at the ready, "Are you not his uncle? Is it not your responsibility?"

"How does the boy learn of his clan if he does not live with his clan?" Awi-e Usdi had retorted, stubbornly glaring up at the tall husband of his sister. His father had been undeterred, ignoring his wife's brother. His uncle had waited stubbornly until his father violently jabbed his spear into the water and then pulled it back with a large fish flopping from the end. Glaring at his father, his uncle had stomped off in disgust.

It had never been discussed in front of him, but he had sensed that his mother's family despised his father. Yona Utana was a solitary man, born of the Bear clan. Ugidahli Unega did not know much about his father's family. Just that they lived in the mountains and stayed to themselves. Traditionally, the members of the Bear clan made medicines for the tribe but Yona Utana seemed indifferent to making medicines. Ugidahli Unega had never seen his father work with the village medicine men or attend any of their functions. Oddly, no one seemed to care, and he had never seen the elders challenge his father in any way. It was as if everyone was afraid of his father and let his father do as he pleased. He had once heard someone say that his father should've been named "Lone Bear" instead of "Great Bear". Ugidahli agreed.

Entering the home the next morning, he found everyone asleep lying around the hearth. Starving, he poured himself a bowl of soup from the pot sitting beside the hearth. Ravenously, he consumed three full bowls.

His poor mother slept soundly, snoring loudly, clearly exhausted. He was a little confused by her extraordinary grief. She had not seemed all that fond of his father and often treated him condescendingly. His mother wasn't a loving person, generally. Awi Ganvnvi, meaning "Deer Track", was outgoing, flighty, and often off track who always needed to be the center of attention. She was constantly chattering, even when she was alone, and always thinking of herself.

Sadly, Ugidahli Unega realized he wasn't very close to either of his parents. He would miss his father, but didn't really feel like grieving, certainly not like his mother.

The image of the lovely nude at the pond took over his thoughts. His father had told him, "All things happen for a reason." What was the meaning of his encounters with the mysterious girl? When the searchers had returned with his father's corpse, she had been there in the strawberry field. When the crowds and his family had abandoned him in front of the village, she alone showed concern for him. And when he had fled from the elders at the dance, she had been there at the pond. His father would have told him, "It could not be a coincidence, seek the meaning, my son."

Maybe she was just a spirit—the messenger of foreboding. He found it strange that he had never noticed her before, but, then, he had not lived in the village. His father had preferred to live outside the village near the banks of the river upstream. In their many disagreements, his father had argued with his mother that it was better to be "free" and that the fishing and hunting was better. Of course, his mother preferred the social aspect of living in the village. So, as a young child, he had only visited the village when his mother had taken him with her on short visits to her family. And then, he had rarely played with any of the other children in the village outside of his cousins. His Cousins. They would probably know the mysterious girl—if she was a girl and not a spirit.

His uncle began to stir. Ugidahli Unega carefully placed his bowl on the hearth and slipped quickly out of the house.

Approaching the home of his favorite cousin, he felt his stomach began to spin. He realized he didn't want to share his secret with anyone. He turned and left the village heading for the pond and waterfall instead.

It was, of course, unlikely that she would be there, but the forlorn boy allowed himself the hope. Stealthily he waded through the thick underbrush and dangling branches and quietly pushed aside the limbs of the forest trees. There it was—the pond where he had found her the night before.

The rising sun illuminated it and the waterfall. Both looked so much smaller in daylight. The chill of the night before was replaced by a steamy heat and the sweet smell of the flowers were overwhelmed by the muggy smell of the leaves and soil being pushed aside by the growing roots. Realizing how close he had been to her made his heart quake. But the pond was empty. His eyes searched all around the pond and found nothing. He pushed into the clearing and found the flat boulder that had betrayed his presence to the nude, bathing beauty. As he made his way to the large rock, he unsuccessfully searched the ground for the guilty stick he had stepped on. Sitting upon the stone lost its appeal now that he was standing by it.

He turned and made his way to the tranquil waters of the pond and listened to the soothing sounds of the waterfall. Soft, damp grass cradled his feet. The early sun warmed his back. Refreshing spray from the waterfall cooled his face. For just a brief moment, his mournful world vanished and he felt normal. The fresh water was so inviting that it was no wonder his temptress had sought it out for a late night escape.

He decided that it would work as well for the morning ritual. Although, all of the villagers seemed to practice the tradition of "going to water" each morning, offering thanks and seeking renewal and cleansing that water provided, his family had rarely participated in the formal ceremony in the village. In fact, he couldn't remember his father ever participating. It had been years since he and his parents had gone to water together as a family. Over time, the practice had been reduced to private bathing.

The inspired boy returned to the flat boulder and kicked off his moccasins. As he did, he heard a snap in the distance. He froze; his heart raced; his arms and fingers grew numb and tingly. Was it her? Breathless and expectant, he leaped to find cover.

His eyes dilated to capture the most obscure evidence; his breathing ceased in order to hear the least sound; muscles taut, ready to react instantly; Ugidahli Unega absorbed the environment's clues, all feeding his acute imagination, his hope. There. In the thickness of the bosk, he could hear hints of something moving through the forest air, the slight swish of cloth against cloth, the whisper of ruffling leaves parting gently to allow passage.

There. Flickering shadows betraying the approach. Then: Shafts of sunlight illuminating the unmistakable sheen of bare skin and a human torso. Dark clusters of the leafy shadows obscured the upper body while thick shrubbery hid the lower body. Then long, thin fingers and a delicate hand pierced the concealing branch foliage, moving the natural veil aside to reveal …

"Uncle?"

"Ugidahli. Where have you been? What are you doing here?"

"I dunno," the exposed and disappointed boy answered sheepishly.

His uncle sternly continued. "You should be with your grieving mother. She needs you at this mournful time, but you have been absent. This is no time to play. Your childhood is over now. It is time to step up and replace the obligations now abandoned by your …" the callused man paused momentarily, as if saying the final word was distasteful, then continued: "father."

"Yes, Uncle." The boy responded, hanging down his head.

The insensitive uncle stared condescendingly at the now obsequious nephew.

"Return to your mother now. Be with her, support her through burial and mourning. I will personally teach you how to support her afterwards."

*Standing ominously
shoulder to shoulder was a
ragged, barrel-chested group
the boy recognized as his
father's family. His mother
whispered behind him,
"Who told them?"*

THE VILLAGE HIGH PRIEST, Uku, whispered his prayers as he led the procession away from the village back to the old home beside the river upstream. Ugidahli Unega and his mother's three brothers carried his father's corpse on their shoulders. The dead man's wife, supported by her tearful sister chanted her dead husband's name loudly and with all the anguish she could muster. To Ugidahli Unega, his mother appeared to be competing with the other women following the procession for who could sound the most grievous.

As the procession approached the old house where his family had previously lived, he noticed stacks of colorful clothing next to the river. The imaginative boy nervously scanned the river for bathers hoping to find the mysterious late-night bather from the pond. There were no bathers in the river.

The procession reached the old house and stopped abruptly. He leaned out to peer around his uncles and the Uku curiously. Standing ominously shoulder to shoulder was a ragged, barrel-chested group the boy recognized as his father's family. His mother whispered behind him, "Who told them?"

Her sister explained, "The chief sent a messenger."

Awi Ganvnvi hissed in disgust.

Ugidahli Unega was struck by the contrast in the families. His father's family was stoic, dry-eyed and his grandmother refrained from grieving or chanting like his mother and aunt.

Without words, Yona Utana's family filed into the small house followed by the Uku and Ganvnvi's family. Next to the stones that had once been the hearth was a rectangular hole dug in the spot where Yona Utana had once preferred to sit. The square hole was lined with flat stones creating a stone tomb for the body. Yona Utana's huge brothers lifted the body of their brother off the shoulders of Ganvnvi's brothers and son and carefully folded the body into its tomb. Yona Utana's family led by his mother, placed pots, clothing, toys, bow and quiver with arrows, blow gun, knives, a crude necklace, dance costumes and beads in the tomb.

Respectfully, Ugi's family stood back to allow his mother's family to deposit their contributions. They were only the dead man's bow and quiver, stone knife, bearskin cape, pipe, and a few clay pots. Ugidahli watched his father's mother, Ugidahli's grandmother, glower at his mother when she upped her wailing a notch—"for show" he suspected.

The Uku flicked water over the tomb with his fingers from a small pot dangling on leather ties from his neck. As he chanted his prayer for safe passage to the upper world, Yona Utana's brothers placed three flat stones to cover the top of the tomb.

The Uku continued. "As the plants feed the animals, and as the plants and animals feed the Tsalagi, so shall the Tsalagi feed the plants our bodies in death."

With that, the families placed token stones on top of the stone cover. To his surprise, his mother placed her stone solemnly and then fell upon the tomb crying loudly and chanting her husband's name desperately.

Yona Utana's mother hissed in disgust in the background. Quietly and humbly, the dead man's brothers filed out of the house. Ugidahli's grandmother paused before her grieving grandson and placed her large, gentle hand beside his face, looked lovingly down on him. She smiled warmly and whispered, "Come see us. You are always welcome."

Then she cradled his head in her large hands and kissed him tenderly on his forehead provoking his mother to wail even louder.

Once outside the "old home place," the Uku led the families into the stream where he had them face east while he looked upward with raised arms. "Sge. Thou Old White Spirit, thou hast relinquished thy protective grasp from Yona Utana's souls, as they have become worthless to you."

The Uku turned his eyes to the family, "Thou must not despair, the fire in the hearth has been left for thee. Thou wilt yet live on. Embrace it."

The Uku placed his hands together and closed his eyes, "In the first upper world, thou White Woman Spirit of Excellence hast prepared the White Tables, and the

White Food abounds over it. The grasping hands of the deceased will be pushed away as it is now for thee. Thou must not despair, the fire in the hearth has been left for thee. Thou wilt yet live on. Embrace it."

The Uku waved his hands over the river, "Sge. The Long Man, thou hast relinquished thy protective grasp from Yona Utana's souls, as they have become worthless to you. Cleanse now the bodies and souls of the family."

The Uku immersed himself in the cleansing waters of the river and the family dutifully immersed themselves as well.

As the family emerged from the waters, the priest looked upon them lovingly and reminded them, "Thou must not despair, the fire in the hearth has been left for thee. Thou wilt yet live on. Embrace life."

He then had them face west and continued, "In the second upper world, thou White Woman Spirit of Excellence has prepared the White Tables and the White Food abounds. The grasping hands of the deceased will be pushed away as it is no longer for him but for thee. Thou must not despair; the fire in the hearth has been left for thee. Thou wilt yet live on. Embrace it."

Again, he waved his hands over the river, "Sge. Long Man, thou hast relinquished thy protective grasp from Yona Utana's souls, as they have become worthless to you. Cleanse now the bodies and souls of the family."

The family immersed again. "Thou must not despair, the fire in the hearth has been left for thee. Thou wilt yet live on. Embrace it."

Then the high priest of the village had them face east again for the prayer to the third upper world. As Ugidahli Unega stood shivering in the cold stream bored by the

Uku's droning on, his eyes wandered to the bank where the villagers stood watching the ceremony. His eyes fell instinctively upon the slender figure dressed in a one-piece, pale buckskin dress standing exactly as she had that day when the dust of the crowd had dissipated around her. The startled boy shook his head and wiped his eyes to look again, but the Uku ordered immersion and his mother's boney hand pushed his head down. When he re-emerged, he tried to catch a glimpse before turning back west, but could not wipe the water draining over his face enough to clear his vision.

After what seemed like an eternity, it was time to face east again. His heart leaped when he found her still standing there. His eyes sought her eyes and they connected. Reflexively, he looked away. In his numbing panic, he looked everywhere except at her, but tried to keep her in his peripheral vision until he felt the strong grip of his mother's fingers forcing him into the water again.

The family turned away from the crowd to receive the blessings of the sixth upper world. Images of the heavenly body of his affections flashed into his consciousness. Her shadowy, nude body shedding the pond waters in the moonlight caused his stomach and loins to tingle. Below the surface of the flowing river, he felt the result of the emotions aroused by the thought of her. He looked down to reassure himself that his indiscretion was hidden from view. He picked up the Uku calling upon "The Long Man" and he quickly plunged into the exhilarating waters hoping to clear thoughts of her from his mind and quell the results of those thoughts from his emotions.

The family rotated back to the east. He took his time wiping the dripping waters from his face. He was determined to not look at her, but his eyes betrayed his command and focused directly on her through his fingers. Visions of her nude body overlayed the sight of her dress. Her penetrating eyes gripped him seductively. He was again aroused.

Desperately he turned his attention to the Uku. The priest's eyes singled him out as he finished the prayer to the seventh upper world. "Thou must not despair, the fire in the hearth has been left for thee. Thou wilt yet live on. Embrace it."

"Sge. Ha, now thou hast come to listen, Thou Long Man, thou helper of the Tsalagi. Thou hast taken a firmer grasp upon our souls. We reach out to thee. We come to bathe our souls in thee."

The Uku then clasped his hands in front of his waist and whispered, "You may remove your unclean clothes now and allow the defiled things to wash downstream so that the Long Man can cleanse and strengthen your souls."

Ugidahli Unega's eyes grew wide and his heart skipped.

The priest seemed to focus on the boy; he reached out his hands again and continued. "The white foam will cling to thy head as thou walk the path of life. The white staff will come into thy extended hand."

Ugidahli Unega glanced about him to see that all of his family members were discretely disrobing in the river and letting their clothes drift downstream. As each finished, they reached out their hands symbolically to the river, The Long Man.

As the Uku continued, the sweating boy quickly pulled off his clothes and released them downstream and extended his hands. He felt naked before the world. He nervously glanced east to see if the crowd was looking at him. To his relief, the congregation was departing; no one was looking toward the family; the girl of his fantasy was gone. But her influence lingered on.

The old Uku ended his blessing with, "The fire of the hearth will be left burning for thee and thy soul has been lifted up successively to the seventh upper world."

The Uku then turned and led the family out of the river. Ugidahli Unega covered himself and fell in behind the families. His father's family each went straight to their individual stack of clothes and began dressing. His mother's family stood before their stacks while his aunt, who alone had placed the clothes earlier, handed each one his or her stack of clothing. As she handed her nephew his stack, she shrieked as he reached to take them thereby exposing himself. Everyone glared at him; their eyes on his indiscretion. His Father's family chuckled and turned away. His mother's brothers expelled short breaths of disgust. His mother grabbed his arm and jerked him around, "Ugidahli Unega. What is that?"

"I dunno," he pleaded.

His giggling aunt stepped in and handed his mother her dress for mourning, "Let me help you with this awful thing." glancing at her nephew with a wink. His mother rolled her eyes at the tattered dress. It truly was a dreadful thing.

Ugidahli Unega sat beside the hearth opposite his mother. Since his humiliation, he had tried to be invisible and avoid his mother … and everyone. It had been an easy task since no one seemed inclined to pay any attention to him anyway. Awi-e Usdi was busily poking the sacred tobacco given to the family by the Uku into the family pipe. He had instructed the family to smoke the special tobacco to "enlighten their eyes so they could bravely face the future." Ganvnvi fingered the beads the Uku had left with her to "comfort her heart."

As Awi-e Usdi sucked on the pipe to get it started, Ugidahli noticed the different smell. It was sweeter smelling than any tobacco smoke he had smelled before. His uncle handed his elder sister the pipe he had lit for her. Ganvnvi took the pipe absently and half-heartedly puffed once on it before handing it to her little sister. As the pipe was passed around the hearth, Ugidahli wondered if he would be offered the pipe. He had never been allowed to smoke be-fore. He watched his uncle, sitting next to him, suck on the pipe deeply, close his eyes and slowly let the smoke escape from his nostrils and pursed lips showing extraordinary pleasure in the exercise. Ugidahli's stomach felt queasy as he inhaled the smoke drifting past him. His uncle passed the pipe to him casually without looking at him. The anxious boy glanced around at his relatives. No one was interested in him. His mouth watered as he imagined the sweet taste he was about to experience. He sucked hard on the pipe, gulping and swallowing as he inhaled the luscious tobacco smoke.

The sweet smoke filled his lungs and provoked an uncontrollable coughing fit. All eyes turned to the gasping boy and the curious onlookers burst into laughter at his expense. No matter how hard he tried, he could not stop coughing and the more desperate he became, the more hilarious his family found his predicament.

His sympathetic aunt finally jumped to her feet and handed her nephew a bowl of water. He gulped it down in desperation. His stomach nauseous and his head spinning, the rookie smoker wiped sweat from his forehead and breathed deeply trying to clear his head.

The laughter had stopped. The family's attention turned back to the hearth. Awi-e Usdi solemnly stood and announced that the family should go to the council house reception. It was obvious that no one was looking forward to an evening of accepting everyone's condolences except for Ugidahli. But, he had no idea what was to happen at the Council house.

As the normally boisterous family rose solemnly, Ugidahli was reminded of a time long, long ago when his father's family had come to visit at their old house. His uncle Ahuli had been invited to play his drum at the ball play dance and his father's family was unusually upbeat and happy during that visit although still not in the category of boisterous. It was one of his earliest memories. He remembered his uncle showing him how he used one hand to control the tone as he used a drumstick to beat it with the other. He remembered crawling up and sitting on his uncle's huge drum to the amusement of everyone. He had been fascinated with this new toy and had accepted the drumstick from his uncle to chew on. It was a happy time.

As his mother's family filed out of his aunt's house and strode down the street, his thoughts lingered on memories of that day when his father's family had filed out of their old house in the forest to go to the village. His father had carried him on his shoulders as the family followed the trail alongside the river. The cool breeze blew his father's hair into his face and it danced and tickled his eyes and nose. His father smelled different that day— clean, not sweaty. He could smell the freshly tanned and fashioned leather of the family's brightly colored clothes. His mother's dress jingled as she walked. He felt the thrill and anticipation of something exciting happening.

He remembered that they had come to a spot where the wide river was calm and they found a number of men standing in the river facing another man. His uncle had announced that they were the opposing team preparing for the game. His father and his brothers approached the ceremony despite the cautionary warnings of his grand-mother. As they approached, three warriors ran up to challenge them. His father and uncles seemed completely oblivious of the threat, held their position and continued to discuss the ceremony amongst themselves even as the warriors extolled them to move on. They finally did move on but in their own time. No one could intimidate his father's family.

His mother's family turned onto the broad avenue that led from the front entrance of the fortress-like village to the Council House and large field that occupied the center of the village. Ugi remembered how huge the village and the avenue had seemed to him back then when he was not much more than a baby. Now the avenue seemed small and inconsequential and the village tight and cramped. He remembered a group of ladies working under the shade of a large porch-like structure. He remembered the smell of fresh corn being ground into a powder on their metates and dried reeds being woven into baskets. The women were working hard but were laughing and talking and having a good time. Now there was a house standing where the structure had been. Drying plants and herbs hung from the small porch in front. The delicious, warm smell of frying bread wafted through the streets just as it had years ago. Young men dressed in lavish dance costumes strolled onto the avenue from a side street followed by young girls carrying turtle-shell rattles. Ugi remembered that the girls danced with the heavy rattles strapped to the legs.

As they approached the Council House, he was sur-prised by how old and unimpressive it appeared now. The Council House sat to the left of the avenue atop a rectangular, flat-topped mound. It was a large, round structure with a steep, pointy roof. A simple portico framed the large door facing the ball play field which lay to the east and opposite the avenue. That night the whole village was assembling on the field where a large delegation was busy building a huge fire while families were staking out their places around the perimeter leaving room for the dancers, just like that night years ago with his father's family. Ugidahli wondered why his father's family had only come that one time.

"Mother, didn't uncle Ahuli used to play the drum for the ball play?"

Ugi's uncles chuckled at his question as if he had told some inside joke. "Oh, just once that I remember," she responded and then chuckled herself.

"Why just once?" he pressed.

His uncle muttered, "His drum was bad medicine."

This comment provoked great laughs from his family. Ugidahli was confused. Awinita put her arm around him and whispered, "The team lost that night."

As the family climbed the seven wide steps up the mound to the Council House portico, Ugi realized that he had never been inside the imposing structure.

It was entered through a small portico on the east side. Flakes of stucco had fallen off the walls where the posts joined the main structure leaving the joints exposed. The naked bark was weathered and smelled dry and old. Ugidahli was surprised that no one had bothered to repair it or even pick up the stucco pieces lying on the ground. Many footsteps had trampled the pieces into the ground and spread them around the opening. Smoke and heat escaped as the reed mat covering the door was pushed aside. The huge room was gloomy and lit only by the sacred fire crackling in the hearth. One continuous bench lined the outside wall. A white bench and a red bench encircled the large hearth in the center of the room where the sacred fire was always burning. An aisle cut through the benches from the door to the hearth and then continued again on the other side. Three red thrones sat to the west of the hearth inside the circular red bench. Three white thrones sat behind the red thrones intersecting the white circular bench.

"Who sits there?" Ugi whispered to this aunt.

"The War Chief; his lieutenant and messenger sit on the Red Thrones. His war council sits on the red benches. The Peace Chief, Uku, and assistant sit on the white thrones and the clan elders and religious leaders sit on the white benches. The common public sits against the wall."

"Where are we going to sit?"

Awinita nodded toward the hearth, "The Uku is coming to escort us to our usual seats."

The unsuspecting boy soon learned why no one had been anxious to go to the Council House reception. An endless stream of well-wishers filed by the family, each stopping to take their hand gently and pausing to express their sympathy and understanding silently.

Ugidahli Unega was yawning broadly when he felt her warm, soft hands clasp his. He gasped in the middle of his yawn reviving another round of coughing. The pretty sympathizer smiled sheepishly, giggled timidly, squeezed and massaged his hand while she waited patiently for the poor boy to recover. Then she moved away gracefully to disappear into the crowd. The excited mourner leaned to follow, but was seized by the boney, bespeckled hand of the next elderly sympathizer.

While enduring the ritual of consoling, the bored young mourner had overheard conversations about the dance that everyone was participating in that night. He learned that the mourning family had their choice whether to attend or not. Once the last person had passed through, he watched with great anticipation to see whether the family headed toward home or toward the dance field. As they left the council house, he decided to take the initiative. "Want to go to the dance, Mother?"

Ganvnvi showed her son a pitiful face, "Oh, I don't think I feel like that tonight. I just want to go home."

With that, she turned away from the devastated boy and headed toward home. To his surprise, he felt his aunt's hand on his shoulder, "Why don't you go, Ugi. Might be good for you."

Ugi's eyes lit up, a broad smile spread across his face, and without waiting for any further discussion, the freed boy raced to the dance field.

He didn't know what to expect at the dance, but he had not expected to be completely ignored. After all, he was the son of the man for which this dance was honoring. As he stood on the sidelines watching the dancers perform, he remembered the colorful costumes that his grandmother had placed in the tomb of his father. He had never known that his father had been a dancer. He wished his father had taught him how to dance so he could join in.

Soon, he became bored. He began searching the dancers and audience for that special girl. But after strolling all around the dance circle and eyeing each person in attendance, she was not to be found. Then it hit him—the pond at the waterfall.

The eager boy, determined to not lose his nerve this time, crashed noisily into the clearing in front of the pond. Once again, the pond was brightly illuminated by the waning moon. He could not accept what he saw. She was not there. Dejectedly he dragged himself over to the flat boulder beside the pond, dropped on to it and propped his chin on his fists. Every sound from the forest attracted his attention. But each ensuing event left him disappointed.

The drums from the dance and the flames from the fire had long since died down and the moon had disappeared behind the trees when he finally dragged himself away from the pond and back to his house where a restless, sleepless night would follow.

*The priest took out his knife
and sliced a sliver of meat
from the bird's bare breast.
He held the meat in front of
his forehead and mumbled a
prayer. Then he looked at
Ugidahli and explained,
"When I drop this in the fire,
if it pops one or more times
and throws small pieces toward
the family, the sons will soon die!"*

WHEN THE NEXT MORNING finally arrived, he overheard his family discussing the days ahead. He was particularly distressed to learn there would be seven days and nights of mourning, each beginning by going to water with the village Uku.

Fortunately, the water ceremony would not be like his first experience. These ceremonies would be a private affair without mourners watching from the banks. He would soon become accustomed to disrobing in front of his family before entering the stream. And he managed to contain his emotions.

The long days dragged on desperately slowly. Neighbors visited often, bringing food and comforting his morose mother. The bereft boy soon understood that his mother didn't need his comfort and did not question his disappearances. Leaving the house gave him moments of freedom and relief from the oppressive mourning ritual.

These brief respites were usually spent leaning against a tree within view of the strawberry patch or sitting on the flat stone by the pond hoping to once again see her; hoping to find the nerve to speak to her; to learn her name; to be with someone who cared about him. But she never came.

On the fifth day of mourning, the Uku returned home with the family after the water ceremony. He sat beside the hearth next to Ganvnvi and chatted pleasantly with her while Awi-e Usdi prepared the pipe with the last of the sacred tobacco. The family passed the pipe around and when it became Ugidahli's turn, Awi-e Usdi shared with the priest, "Ugidahli Unega has found the tobacco very disagreeable."

The family laughed as the High Priest smiled knowingly at the boy. Ugidahli gritted his teeth and glared at his uncle.

Undeterred, his uncle cautioned, "Be careful this time."

Taunted by everyone's laughter, this time he puffed briefly without inhaling and passed it on. His uncle persisted, "What's the matter Ugi, afraid of a little smoke?"

Awinita stepped in, "I remember the first time I smoked the pipe! I was nauseous for a week," she giggled. Ugi smiled gratefully as he caught her eye. *Why couldn't everyone be like her? How did such a loving and understanding person come from this family? How could she be his mother's sister?*

When the pipe returned to Awi-e Usdi, the Uku became very grave as he pulled a dead bird from a pouch attached to his waist belt. As the priest plucked the feathers off the right breast of the bird, he explained that he was upholding a long practiced tradition. Often families worried about their own longevity after a death and this ritual could confirm or dispel their anguish.

The priest took out his knife and sliced a sliver of meat from the bird's bare breast. He held the meat in front of his forehead and mumbled a prayer. Then he looked at Ugidahli and explained, "When I drop this in the fire, if it pops one or more times and throws small pieces toward the family, the sons in the family will soon die. If it does not pop, they …" the kindly Uku smiled at him, "… you are safe."

The startled son's eyes grew big and round to the amusement of the family and priest. The Uku tossed the sliver into the fire. At first, nothing happened and then it ignited a great, white, sparkling flame. Everyone gasped as Ugidahli looked expectantly at the priest who seemed to be stunned by the event. "I've never seen that before." he muttered.

All were silent as he pondered that event and then declared, "Well, it didn't pop, did it?"

The family celebrated with hoots and applause as the embarrassed boy smiled proudly. It was nice to know he wouldn't be dying soon.

The first five days and nights of mourning were just a foggy blur to Ugidahli. He had just allowed himself to exist long enough for the ordeal to end, but he dreaded the ending, for then he would have to begin training with his mean uncle.

The next two days took a different, scary turn. After going to water, the family returned to the tomb of Yona Utana where they joined the local women who set up a most bitter wailing, chanting Yona Utana's name over and over and over … for what seemed like forever to the poor, frightened son.

Afterwards, the men, the hunters of the village, met the returning family and presented them with game they had killed for the occasion. Ganvnvi thanked them graciously. Well, more than graciously, elaborately. Well, more than elaborately, exceedingly. So much so, that her embarrassed family pulled her away and nodded apologetically to the hunters.

Backing away, they bumped into the massive and immovable brothers of Yona Utana who stood with deer carcasses draped over their shoulders. Ganvnvi examined the large men and their prize and muttered, "Oh … dear."

Yona Utana's mother and oldest brother then appeared with a pot of corn, squash, and beans, a popular soup generally known as "Three Sisters."

Ganvnvi put her hand to her mouth and mouthed, "Oh, my …"

Ugidahli Unega beamed at his grandmother who returned a loving smile to her skinny grandson.

The village peace chief interrupted the awkward moment by encouraging the village to proceed to the Council House for a feast. Ganvnvi immediately broke out of her spell and loudly repeated the chief's proclamation. "Yes, yes, everyone, please join us for a great feast."

As she led the procession and rattled on, Ugidahli Unega stumbled over to his grandmother and hugged her around her bounteous waist. She beamed a bright smile and responded, "Come on, Grandson, we have a feast to prepare."

*A wavy, ethereal image
standing on a stone pinnacle
materialized before him.
It was his father. The
ghostly figure looked down
with the familiar distant
look in his eyes.*

They had been hiding in the midst of the leafy bushes since before sunrise. The fresh coolness of the morning had long since burned off as the sun climbed high into the sky. The crisp honey-like smell of the bush mixed with wet grass had been replaced by the clammy stench of sweaty hunters. Flies teased Ugidahli by landing on his face and swiping themselves with their hairy limbs. He was forbidden to shoo the flies since it might spook a deer.

Bored and frustrated, Ugidahli sat next to his intense uncle waiting for the deer that would never come. He had been justified to dread these lessons and now, after almost a half moon cycle, he was convinced that his uncle had nothing more to teach him. It was always the same. Spend several days staking out an area where his uncle found signs of deer. Then, when they didn't return, move to another equally unlikely area.

On those rare occasions when a deer actually did wander by, Uncle Awi-e Usdi would adeptly string his arrow and shoot the deer while his frustrated student fumbled with his bow. He could see that he was never going to learn how to bag a deer as long as his uncle found great pleasure in showing him up.

On this, the fourteenth day, as the long hot day slowly passed, Ugidahli cooked up a plan.

Three drops of blood on the yellow petals of an awiakta, "deer eye", flower had been the last indication to Ugidahli that he was on the right trail. Now, Sister Sun was on her way down the sky vault and if he did not find the deer soon, he would not be able to return home before dark— the mistake that may have cost his father his life. He squatted to examine the prints in the soft forest ground. He checked the plants, the ground, the rocks but found no blood. As much as he hated it, he must now admit that the deer had not been mortally wounded and he would not be able to catch up to it. The despondent boy sat back, placed his elbows on his knees and buried his face in his palms.

Sneaking out of the house early that morning, he had purposefully missed his uncle. This was to be the day that he would find and kill a deer on his own and bring it home in triumph. This was to be the day that he would show his uncle and show his mother, that he no longer needed his ruthless uncle anymore. He hated his stern, taskmaster uncle who showed him no kindness and gave him no comfort since the loss of his father. And he hated his father for dying and leaving him alone.

He had been so proud of himself for finding the deer, but, in his eagerness and excitement, he had spooked the deer and his arrow had missed the mark. Now it was clear that the deer had been only slightly wounded and he would have to return home in shame.

The humiliated hunter lowered his head and whispered, "Forgive me, deer, I am a bad shot and not worthy of your meat. Hear my prayer, Awi Usdi, may your brother deer, that I have wronged, heal and live long."

Practically the only worthwhile thing he had learned from his uncle was about Awi Usdi, "Little Deer", a small, invisible deer that kept constant protective watch over his subjects, and saw to it that not one was ever killed in wantonness. When a deer was shot by the hunter, Little Deer knew it at once and was instantly at the spot to ask the blood stains of the slain deer if the hunter had asked pardon for the life he had taken. If not, Little Deer delivered crippling and painful rheumatism to the murderer.

As the despondent hunter made his way down the mountain, long shadows darkened his path and he realized that he would not be able to get home before dark. Pangs of fear overcame him. He shivered at the horrible vision of his dead father's mutilated body being carried into the village. Anger boiled in him. He raised his fist to the upper world where his father must now be and screamed, "How could you let this happen?"

A wavy, ethereal image standing on a stone pinnacle materialized before him. It was his father. The ghostly figure looked down with the familiar distant look in his eyes. Not hateful but not loving; not imposing but not inviting. The same aloofness that had always left Ugidahli unsure of his father's feelings and afraid to approach him. Ugidahli raised his arm slowly to wave, but the image began fading away.

"Why?" Ugidahli screamed. "Can't you just acknowledge that I exist?"

The boy's anger fired ever greater as he bounded up the slope toward the vanishing image determined to attack his thoughtless father for leaving him; for never giving him the love he so desperately craved all his life; for abandoning him and leaving him to endure the disdain of his mother's family. The steep, slippery base of the pinnacle proved insurmountable forcing him to face the reality that it was useless to continue and whatever he had seen, had vanished. Exhausted and heart-broken, he collapsed and allowed his limp body to slide down the slope.

He curled up at the dusty base of the pinnacle letting his mixed emotions play out. Grief brought forth self-pity and tears. Then anger drove him to sit up, grit his teeth, clench his fists and proclaim, "I don't need you! I don't need anyone!"

The angry boy dusted himself off and wiped muddy tears from his face. It was getting dark now and he must continue his return through the forest.

When he came to one of the many streams he had crossed that day, he remembered an old hut he had passed earlier that morning. The hut sat next to a flowing stream just over the hill from this one. Maybe he could spend the night there. The hut had looked empty, but if someone lived in it, he hoped he would be friendly and have food. He had not eaten anything all day prompting him to imagine deer meat roasting on a spit over the fire. The fear that had settled in his stomach that had been replaced with anger was now replaced with pangs of hunger.

He glanced up to see two, large ravens that appeared to sparkle as if on fire. As they glided over the trees, his vision of the birds was interrupted by the leaves and branches causing them to flicker and appear distorted. The image of a man transposed over one raven while the other alternated appearing as a woman.

T HE HUNGRY HUNTER ANNOUNCED his approach with a growling stomach. Twilight was melting the long shadows and a haze was slowly building. He could feel the dank wetness of the approaching stream and could smell the foul stench of rotting fish and frog slime. A hut with several out buildings was nestled in the thick grove of trees beyond a small field planted with corn, beans, and squash.

As he waded across the shallow, narrow pond, he noticed that it was not the usual hut. It was, instead, a seven-sided house; more like a small council house than a residence. However, the usual round, mud-packed asi used for warmth in the winter or ceremonial cleansing year-round bulged like a mushroom next to the house and a square corn hut on stilts stood next to the corn-field confirming to him that it was, indeed, a residence.

Squawking ravens overhead interrupted his perusal of the odd compound. He glanced up to see two, large ravens that appeared to sparkle as if on fire. As they glided over the trees, his vision of the birds was interrupted by the leaves and branches causing them to flicker and appear distorted. The image of a man transposed over one raven while the other alternated appearing as a woman. It was a peculiar phenomenon that the boy had never witnessed before. It was as if, as they passed over the trees, the sun shimmering off the leaves was playing tricks on his eyes. Then, the strange ravens dove through the window of the seven-sided house.

Unsettled by the mysterious event, he rubbed his eyes and looked again at the window, questioning his senses. He waited for further evidence to confirm what he thought he had just seen but nothing moved in the house and the normal sounds of the forest resumed around him. His curiosity pushed him to investigate. Stealthily, he approached the house.

An old, hefty, but nimble woman bounded out of the house carrying a large, empty basket. The smile on her face and the twinkle in her eye suddenly turned to alarm as she abruptly braked to a stop and glared at the stranger before her.

The nervous boy appealed to the startled woman, "Osiyo, Grandmother. I am Ugidahli Unega of the Deer Clan. My mother is Awi Ganvnvi and I am from the village of Toruro."

Overwhelmed, it seemed the old woman grew larger as she stood unflinching with dark eyes fixed on the intruder. She seemed curiously familiar, but he was sure he had never seen her before. Squinting her eyes, it was as if she was trying to determine if he was whom he said he was.

He continued, "I have been tracking a deer that I … wounded this morning and now it is getting late and I will not be able to get home before dark."

Still the grand woman stood firm, making him more nervous as he continued. "I was hoping you might let me stay here tonight. I will not be a burden on you."

The old woman spun around and scurried back into the odd house without answering. Flustered, he debated what to do. Maybe he should continue on and hope to find another place to spend the night. Maybe he should patiently wait to see if the old woman would change her mind.

He heard the door cover rustle. Cautiously, a tall, thin old man shuffled out and approached him, "Siyo."

"Siyo." He answered timidly.

"Ajilusgi tells me you are a hunter needing shelter for the night?"

"*Ajilusgi*"? The incredulous young hunter tried desperately to resist the urge to giggle. The rugged, huge woman did not remind him of a "Flower." Refocusing, "Yes, Grandfather, I have spent too much time tracking the deer I only wounded this morning. Now I will not be able to get home before dark and I am afraid ..."

The old man chuckled. "Come in, hunter. We will give you shelter ... from the dark ..."

With that, the jovial old man turned and headed back into his house. Frustrated, Ugidahli wanted to explain that he feared the fate of his father, not the dark, but realized he had missed his opportunity and gratefully followed the old man into his house.

When he entered the house, the smell hit him like a strong wind. Sweet smells, spicy smells, putrid smells, all meshed together in startling crispness that took his breath away. The house was littered with bowls, jars and baskets full of potions, plants, insects, and the bones, skins and dissected parts of animals.

"What's all of this for?" he blurted out while waving his hand to indicate all of the mysterious concoctions.

The old couple looked at each other anxiously. "Flower" fidgeted as she studied her husband, the old man pointed to his wife and then himself and muttered, "We are Kuni-akati. We make medicine for and to treat wounded warriors."

Ugidahli Unega had never heard of a "Kuni-akati", but had seen medicine men and the Uku treat people before. He was familiar with their use of strange medicines and potions. He had never seen inside one's house, however. He was fascinated and although he was of the Ani Kawi, the Deer clan, one of his cousins was of the Ani Sahoni, the Blue Holly clan, and they kept medicinal gardens and made herbs and medicines for children. However, they had nothing like this.

"All of this for wounded warriors?" he queried.

The old man seemed agitated, "Ajilusgi will prepare something to eat. Are you hungry?"

"Oh, yes, Grandfather," he answered respectfully.

Ajilusgi ignored her husband and addressed her guest. "You live in the village of Tororu?"

"Yes, Grandmother," again using the term for respect.

The imposing woman continued to study him and it was making him very uncomfortable. *Did she not believe him? Did she not like the village?* Something was bothering the old woman.

Finally, she appeared to come to some conclusion and put her fists on her hips, cocked her head to one side and allowed a slight smirk to accompany her challenging eyes, "You did not mention your father."

Ugidahli Unega looked down sadly. "My father is dead. He was attacked by night predators while carrying back a deer carcass one night."

He glanced up to see the old woman raise one eyebrow as she turned to her husband. The couple nodded their heads knowingly. They were looking at each other with an expression that told him that maybe now they understood his fear of the night. Unbeknownst to him, of course, it was not what they were thinking at all.

The old man gestured toward the hearth, "Come sit. Ajilusgi has been preparing some very nice … venison for us. Tell me about your hunt."

Ugidahli joined the old man by the hearth and as he began his story, the old man prepared a pipe.

"Well, since my father died, my uncle has been teaching me how to hunt."

He paused while he decided how much he should tell this stranger, but there was something about the old man that put him at ease. He seemed like a kind man. Inexplicably, he wanted to confide in him, "My uncle is a mean man. I don't like hunting with him."

The old man looked up at the boy as he tamped the tobacco down in the bowl of the pipe. Without comment, nor any other discernible reaction, the old man reached for a splint and lit it from the hearth flame. Uncomfortable, the boy shifted and continued, "I wanted to prove to him … and Mother that I didn't need him anymore, so I slipped out before dawn by myself to hunt. About the time Sister Sun climbed above the trees, I spotted a nice deer. I quickly asked its forgiveness and then shot it."

The old man raised his eyebrows as he sucked on the pipe to get it started. Clouds of sweet smelling smoke billowed out of his mouth and swirled around his head. He nodded to prod the boy along, "I was not patient and spooked the deer. My arrow missed the mark and the deer bolted into the forest."

The old man handed him the pipe and sat back patiently. He was apprehensive as he accepted the pipe. He remembered his first experience with smoking tobacco and feared a repeat in front of his new friends. Carefully, he drew on the pipe and quickly blew the smoke out. Satisfied that he had successfully fulfilled his obligation, he handed the pipe back to his host, "I have been tracking the deer all day, but there has been no blood in the trail since this morning." Again the young hunter bowed his head sadly, "I only wounded him."

The old man held the pipe in his lap as he waited for the boy to finish. After a polite moment, he raised the pipe to his mouth and sucked thoughtfully on the pipe. The boy interrupted, "I followed the deer too long."

The old man quickly handed the pipe back. "When I realized that I would not be able to get home before dark, I was very worried."

He looked down at the pipe in his hand and tried to hand it back to his host as he continued, "After what happened to my father … well, I didn't want to take a chance."

The old man frowned and pushed the pipe back again. He looked at the pipe curiously. He didn't want to risk another cough fit, but he could see that the old man was insisting. He looked back at the old man, not sure what to do or what was wrong. The troubled host queried, "Do you not like the tobacco?"

The boy suddenly realized that he had insulted his generous host. "No, Grandfather, the tobacco is very good."

The old man was silent obviously waiting for an explanation, "I … uh … well, I am not accustomed to smoking. I did not mean to offend you."

The old man chuckled as he reached for the pipe, sat back and drew on it and watched the smoke swirl as he exhaled. Then he looked back at the boy, "It is customary for the one with the pipe to speak. When he hands the pipe to someone else, then he is indicating that he is through speaking and the other may speak."

Ugidahli was embarrassed by his ignorance and blushed as the veteran and his wife cackled at him. Their infectious laughter drew him in and the three strangers experienced a connection that, as it would turn out, be a lifetime friendship.

As Ajilusgi set the slab of meat on a spit over the fire, the old man enjoyed his pipe. Ugidahli sat quietly, respectfully waiting for him to speak, "We have been poor hosts. I am Galonedv Adutlvdodi, Adawehi, Ani Wodi, Paint Clan. Yona Gunuge, Ajilusgi, is of the Ani Yona, Bear Clan."

The boy was proud to be treated as an adult by his new friends. He beamed a broad smile at Ajilusgi and started to speak, but caught himself. Adawehi smiled and passed him the pipe. Embarrassed, he took the pipe and quickly inhaled burning his chest and setting off a dreaded coughing event. Ajilusgi impulsively dipped a bowl in the pot of water next to the hearth and handed it to the gasping guest who gulped down the water frantically only provoking his choking lungs. Ajilusgi grabbed his shoulder with a surprisingly firm grip and pounded his back with her other large, meaty hand.

At first, assuming he was being punished for his rudeness, he struggled hard to control his demeaning convulsion. But, as she began to alternately rub and pat his back and whisper soothingly, "Relax, take a slow, deep breath, relax ..."

He realized that her attention was relieving his lungs and as he relaxed and took deep breaths his seizures ceased. Finally, he was able to take a deep, unobstructed breath and totally relax. His hosts smiled supportively as they waited for him to recover.

A moment of awkward silence was relieved by Adawehi, "You were about to speak ..."

Ugidahli's face contorted as he strained to recollect what he had intended to say. Nothing came to mind.

Ajilusgi pulled a large flint-knapped knife from a leather scabbard. The boy flinched as she reached over him and cut a sliver of meat. She handed it to the skittish guest and proceeded to slice pieces for herself and her husband. She placed a large clay pot on the edge of the hearth in the embers, "Three Sisters soup," she explained as she handed out soup bowls.

Adawehi tapped the inverted bowl of his pipe on the side of the hearth stones to empty it of ashes and then stored it next to him. He appeared to be deep in thought as he gnawed at his sliver of meat.

"Patience," he proclaimed prophetically.

Ugidahli Unega listened politely but Adawehi did not elaborate. The boy studied the word. *Yes, I should be patient when I smoke. 'Relax' and take my time. I will be sure to do so next time,* he thought.

"What are you babbling about?" Ajilusgi challenged her husband.

Adawehi patiently smiled at his wife, "Hunting deer."

The young hunter stared quizzically at the old sage.

"You must be very patient when hunting. You must think as a deer; study him very closely. Look into his eyes and understand what he is thinking."

Ugidahli's uncle had never told him this. "How do you know what he's thinking, Grandfather?"

Adawehi smiled omnisciently, "Put yourself in his place. Watch where he is looking. Think about what he sees and what you would think in his place. Study his muscles. Are they tense? Is he relaxed? Watch his nostrils. Is he smelling something in the air?"

The novice hunter was mesmerized. He could immediately see the merit in what the old man was suggesting.

Adawehi continued, "If you see that he is tense and he is sniffing the air, then he senses he is in danger. If it is the hunter he is sensing, be very still. If it is something else, you may be in danger, as well. Follow his eyes. See where he is looking. Use him to determine your own safety."

The inexperienced hunter loved this. For the first time in his life, he wanted to go hunting. "Will you take me hunting, Grandfather?"

Adawehi and Ajilusgi laughed heartily. He shrunk back. *What did I say? Why is that funny?* He wondered.

Ajilusgi sensed his apprehension, "Adawehi is honored you would want to go hunting with him. But, at our age, these things are more difficult."

Understanding, the boy smiled broadly and relaxed and resumed chewing on his venison. His hosts resumed eating as well. He looked about the large heptagonal room. *All this for a wounded warrior,* he reflected.

"It sure takes a lot to care for a wounded warrior."

The old Kuni-akati's appeared to be unsettled by the boy's observation. They watched with concern as the curious guest stood and walked over to one of the many pots lining the outer walls of the house. "What is this for?"

Adawehi glanced at his frowning wife, took a deep breath and replied, "Each herb is seldom used by itself to treat the afflicted. They must be mixed with other herbs or animal extracts. And when they are administered, they must be accompanied by the proper conjure or prayer to work properly."

"Conjure?"

"Medicine is about our relationship with the living earth, earth's creatures and plants, and the spirits. A plant reaches into mother earth for nourishment and can extend its relationship to us when administered properly. Each plant reaches out to Sister Sun and to the air around it and absorbs the rain. It has the potential, then, to extend each of these relationships to those who know how to acquire them. When the animals eat plants, that relation-ship is extended to them. When we eat the animals, the relationships are extended. The conjure calls to those relationships and brings them out."

The boy was fascinated by the old man's wisdom. He glanced about the room at the myriads of plants, animal parts, powders, lotions and liquids. Adawehi sensed that the boy was at once curious and confused. As he reached for his pipe and tobacco pouch, he invited the curious boy, "Come sit with me and let me tell you a story."

The boy dutifully joined the old story teller. Adawehi seemed to be pleased by his youthful curiosity. He noted that Ajilusgi was as well. She had taken up a seat next to the inquisitive boy and her sad eyes looked upon the boy tenderly. He was a little unnerved by her curious change of heart. "Got any children?"

Her voice quivered as she replied, "We have not been blessed with children."

Adawehi was staring longingly into the fire as he whispered, "We have been punished for our choices."

The saddened man forced a smile and looked at the boy, "Having you visit us has brought mixed blessings. But, right now in this moment, the void left in our childless lives is temporarily overflowing."

The old wizard, whose clan had faithfully preserved the stories and sacred teachings of the Cherokee, the "real" people, took his time, enjoyed his pipe. Ugidahli's anticipation was growing. Did it always take old people forever to start a story? It sure seemed like it. The old man began his story, "In the ancient times, birds, fishes, insects, animals, and even plants could talk to each other. All things lived in harmony and peace. But as time passed, human beings increased so rapidly that the animals began to feel cramped. To make matters worse, the human beings created weapons to slaughter the animals, birds, and fishes for food and skins. And the smaller creatures like frogs and worms were carelessly trampled by these disrespectful people. So, the animals decided to council."

Ugidahli loved stories. Adawehi glanced at him out of the corner of his eye. His eye appeared to sparkle and the corner of his mouth turned up slightly. Ajilusgi involuntarily reached for the boy's head, then caught herself and withdrew dolefully. He felt a pang in his heart for this old couple who appeared to so much need a child in their lives.

Adawehi continued, "The bears were the first to council on the Kuwahi Mountain, the 'Mulberry place,' and the old White Bear chief presided. He allowed each to relate how Man had killed their friends for food and skins and concluded they should declare war against Man. They knew that they were no match for Man's bow, but it was determined that their claws were too long to be able to shoot a bow and if they cut off their claws, they would not be able to hunt and feed themselves. It was plain to them that Man's weapons were not intended for them. So, the old White Bear dismissed the council and they returned to the woods.

"Next, the Deer held council under their chief, Awi Usdi. They were sympathetic toward Man, but were hurt that man did not respect them. Awi Usdi decided that they would send rheumatism to every hunter that did not ask their pardon before killing one of them."

He smiled and Adawehi caught the subtle smile on his listener's lips. He had learned about this curse. Ajilusgi stood, set the pot of Three Sisters soup off the coals and waddled off appearing to be busy, but to Ugidahli, she was just shuffling things around mindlessly.

"The Fishes and Reptiles held their council and determined to make their victims dream of snakes twining about them in slimy folds and blowing foul breath in their faces, or make them dream of eating raw or decaying fish, so that they would lose appetite, sicken and die.

"Finally, the Birds, Insects, and smaller animals came together. Each one was allowed to speak and in the end, they voted Man to be guilty. They then began to devise so many diseases for Man that had not their invention at last failed them, no one of the human race would have been able to survive."

The boy frowned angrily. Perhaps he had misjudged the birds, insects and small animals. Perhaps he should not be so nice to them. Adawehi continued.

"When the plants, who were friendly with Man, heard what the animals had devised, they determined to defeat their evil designs. Each Tree, Shrub, and Herb, even down to the Grasses and Mosses, agreed to furnish a cure for each one of the diseases devised."

As the raconteur refreshed his pipe, the curious listener pondered the story. Then he asked, "So how do you know which plant will help with which disease?"

Smoke surrounded the medicine man's head as he lowered his pipe to explain, "The spirit of the plant will tell me when I ask."

Adawehi smiled at the boy knowingly, "But, that is a skill that takes a lifetime to master. Children of my clan begin learning of the plant's gifts as soon as we learn to talk. We learn to ask for the plant's powers through the conjures."

Ugidahli frowned. He was of the Ani Kawi clan. It was probably too late for him to start learning about these things. Clan tradition would prohibit him, as well. Then, he remembered something. His eyes darted around the room, "Where are the flaming ravens?"

Ajilusgi gasped audibly. Adawehi choked on his pipe. Ajilusgi exclaimed harshly, "What are you talking about, child?"

The child could see that his inquiry had triggered a nerve. The stout woman stood imposingly over the shy boy with her fists pressing her rotund hips; her dark eyes glared at him piercing his skin. He felt his body shrinking into itself, "I dunno." he whimpered.

His utter supplication shocked his hosts and they involuntarily burst into uncontrollable laughter. It was obvious that he had no idea the gravity and implication of his question. The great woman whisked up the boy in her bounteous arms and hugged him grandly.

But the levity of the moment could not cover the dire portents of his question. Something in their eyes told him that they sorely wanted to forget about the subject.

Ugidahli Unega had never seen anything like it—it was truly beautiful. As he took the necklace he looked apprehensively into the old man's stern eyes, "Take this to remember us. But it is also a reminder that it is our wish that you never speak of what you have seen here or of us to anyone."

THE STENCH OF THE house, the presence of new friends, the overwhelmingly exciting new subject and information kept Ugidahli Unega awake well into the night. The conversations of the evening kept cycling over and over in his mind. He wanted to remember every detail; every emotion; every action and reaction of his hosts. This was the most important evening of his life. Ajilusgi's reaction to "Flaming Ravens" puzzled him. He never did find out where the ravens disappeared to. Why was his question so disturbing? He was unaware of when his thoughts slipped into dreams, so when he abruptly awoke to a bright, empty room, he was shocked.

Still struggling to break from the grasp of sleepiness, he got up, rubbed his eyes, and headed outside. He found Adawehi and Ajilusgi standing in the river with hands raised to the rising sun. His mind flashed back to his father's funeral and going to water with the Uku and the thrill of that specter, his eidolon, beckoning him from the shore. The captivated boy squeezed his eyes shut and pursed his lips as the image of his humiliation replaced his fantasy.

His face flushed and he clenched his fists as he desperately tried to force his ignominy from his thoughts.

Today he would be going home. He dreaded returning to his pitiful life now after briefly tasting this exciting and strange world. He felt like he had received more love from these strangers in one night than he had received from his family his whole life. What if he didn't go home? What if he just adopted Adawehi and Ajilusgi and lived with them from now on? He sensed that they had enjoyed visiting with him. They seemed genuinely attached to him.

But what about her? Could he give up the chance that he might see her again? His good senses told him that Adawehi and Ajilusgi would not really accept him. He knew down deep that staying here was just a fantasy—probably like the illusive beauty, two eidolons desired but untouchable.

Adawehi and Ajilusgi seemed distant through breakfast. They were hospitable and courteous but not warm and friendly like they had been the night before. Ugidahli was also quiet. He was sad that he would be leaving.

After breakfast, Ajilusgi presented her guest with a small pouch filled with cornbread cakes for his journey. She smiled tenderly as he accepted her thoughtful gift. He looked up at the large, big-hearted woman sheepishly and she drew him in for a warm hug.

"Maybe I could stay awhile," he blurted out desperately.

She hugged him tighter and then pushed him back. She didn't answer verbally, but he saw the answer in her eyes.

Adawehi reached between them, gently gripped the boy's shoulder and turned him toward the door. With his arm around the boy's shoulder, the unsteady old man walked the reluctant boy outside.

Adawehi handed the boy an unusual necklace. A clear, three-faceted crystal was encased in a netted circle. A leather strap was threaded through the circular pocket and flanked by ten bear claws, five on each side, each separated by colorful beads. A white agate dangled from one side of the bottom of the crystal enclosure and a black agate dangled from the other side. Ugidahli Unega had never seen anything like it—it was truly beautiful. As he took the necklace, he looked apprehensively into the old man's stern eyes, "Take this to remember us. But it is also a reminder that it is our wish that you never speak of what you have seen here or of us to anyone."

Ugidahli was confused. Why did they want to be a secret? His gifter must have read his question on his face, "To preserve the purity of the medicines, no bad spirits should come around to contaminate them."

The boy looked at the extraordinary necklace and considered the old man's plea. "I will keep your secret, Grandfather."

The old man smiled and patted the boy's shoulder. "Return to your mother now. She will be worried about you."

"I want to come back and learn more about the ku … kuni …"

The old man frowned, "You are of the Ani Kawi. Your people are the keepers of the deer. It is a vital responsibility to the Tsalagi. Learn the ways of your clan well and follow the white path of development. Forget us. Our ways are not for you."

Ugidahli looked back at the sad old woman clutching the door frame and then back at the determined old man as he released the boy's shoulder. The boy understood that this was intended to be good bye forever.

Sister Sun was high in the sky dome when Ugidahli Unega reached the bottom of the last hill before reaching his village. He stopped to reconnoiter. The village seemed quiet and no one was stirring outside the palisade walls. He dreaded facing his mother. He dreaded her shame and disappointment in him. He dreaded the mean glare of his uncle. He was certain that Awi-e Usdi would now be twice as stringent.

After his beguiling encounter with the old couple, the Kuni-akati, returning to his dreary life was almost unbearable. Why couldn't he have been born of the Aniwodi? Or even the Anisohoni clan like his cousins? *Wasn't it far more important to save lives than to take them? Or, than to protect a bunch of dumb ole' deer?*

A breeze moved by and made the shadows of the tree leaves dance in his eyes temporarily blinding him. He instinctively moved forward to escape the irritating blindness when he was halted by a shout from behind, "Ugidahli Unega."

It was his uncle's voice. Ugidahli Unega wheeled around, "You are safe," his uncle gasped as he grabbed the startled boy up in his arms. "You are safe," he cried again.

Ugidahli was confused. This could not be his uncle. His uncle had no compassion. His uncle would not worry about him. His uncle didn't even like him.

"We must hurry to your mother. She is weak from worry. She feared that you had joined your father."

Ugidahli Unega would never see the tenderness his uncle had shown that day again. But, because of that day, his uncle's harshness seemed easier to tolerate. At least he knew that his uncle had feelings.

His mother's concern and affection were also short lived. But for that short time, he was given a glimpse of how life could be. Too soon, however, it was back to "normal" and he found himself in the woods again with a stern uncle and living with a mother whose concerns and attention were turned elsewhere.

And, unbeknownst to him, the fascination that had captured his imagination that fateful night with a strange couple had changed his life forever. It had started him down the dark path that would eventually lead to who he would become.

"I want to hunt alone now,"
he stammered.

Tʜɪs ᴍᴏʀɴɪɴɢ, ꜰʀᴜsᴛʀᴀᴛᴇᴅ ʙʏ the previous day's hunting episode, Awi-e Usdi stomped into the forest determined to teach his smart-alecky nephew a thing or two. A confident, smiling Ugidahli Unega trailed behind his dumb uncle triumphantly.

Motivated to be rid of his uncle, the conspiring young hunter had sucked in the knowledge from his uncle and practiced his craft with the enthusiasm of a driven man. He had spent long evenings practicing stringing his arrow quickly and smoothly and firing accurately at his target. He had practiced doggedly until pulling his arrow from its sheath, stringing it into his bow, pulling back and firing was all one fluid motion. In the field, he had challenged his uncle as if in a life-or-death contest which had soon frustrated his uncle. And the more frustrated his uncle became, the more determined he became to show up his nephew and the more determined his nephew became to vanquish his teacher.

Ugidahli was surprised to learn how little his uncle had to offer and how insecure he was when pushed. The young hunter had, at first, wondered when his presumed experienced uncle would teach him the lessons of patience and understanding that Adawehi had shared with him. But, in time, he came to realize that it was a lesson his uncle had yet to learn. Using his secret to advantage, he had, for three days-in-a-row, out-hunted his uncle.

While Awi-e Usdi marched through the forest obstinately, his nephew advanced stealthily behind him with all of his senses called to attention. He could hear every sound of the forest; smell every odor distinctly; taste the forest and its creatures on the breeze; feel every sway of the tree, flicker of leaf, or change in the currents of the air; and detect even the buzz of a nearby gnat.

He halted. There it was in the distant glade disturbed by his uncle's undisciplined clamoring through the brush. It was a magnificent elk.

The covert hunter froze and studied the elk's eyes whose gaze was directed to his uncle. The elk's muscles tightened, and he was ready to bolt. His nostrils flared as he raised his nose slightly. Ugidahli glanced back at his uncle who was oblivious of the elk as he crashed forward on his quest.

Excited by the incredible opportunity, the skilled young predator squatted and kept his eye on his game. The elk would ignore everything else as long as his brash uncle had his attention. He could see that the elk was starting to relax. Even the elk could see that his uncle was clueless and not a serious threat. Carefully the cunning hunter glided quietly through the underbrush and approached his target undetected until the elk's right ear swiveled in his direction. The attentive hunter froze. The elk's eyes darted in his direction as he sniffed for more clues. Satisfied that the uncle was his only threat, the grand elk refocused.

The student pulled back his silently strung arrow, judged the wind, adjusted, and released. The elk looked back just as the arrow penetrated its heart. The lacerated prey lunged back on its folding hind legs and dropped dead to the ground.

"Ugidahli. Nephew. Where are you?" the startled uncle shouted upon realizing he was on a singular campaign.

The nephew bounded down the hill to the glade as he shouted back, "Here, Uncle. Come help me dress my elk."

As the overjoyed young hunter drew his knife, grabbed the elk's antlers, and jerked its head back, he glanced up to see his infuriated uncle shaking his fist and shouting at the top of his lungs. The conquering hunter smiled as he sliced through the dead animal's jugular.

Sister Sun was well on her way home when Ugidahli Unega reached the village. Numerous children playing by the river interrupted their happy games to come running alongside and taunt the triumphant hunter dragging the curious make-shift sled filled with huge, meaty sections of the elk he had slain. Even after decapitation, removing the elk's lower limbs, skinning and degutting it, the huge carcass of the elk had been too much for the boy to carry alone. But he was determined to return home with his prize in triumph. Taking the hide, he fashioned a sled with two long poles. He cut the right flank and then the left and laid them on the sled. Testing it, he quickly found he could easily drag it across the ground. He continued to add dissected sections to the load until it reached his limit.

Villagers began to file through the village entrance attracted by the reveling children's shouts. As he pushed through the growing crowd and approached the village entrance, his mother and aunt appeared. His mother blinked her puffy eyes in the bright sunlight and tried to shade them with her hand. She had been crying. He knew that his uncle had long since returned to complain to her about the morning hunt. He was certain that his uncle's version was not the triumphant story that he would have told.

Aunt Awinita led his mother out to view the spectacle her son had created. She forced a tight smile for her son as she stopped beside him and then surveyed the sled. Surprised by the bounteous meat on the sled, her eyes gleamed proudly as she looked around at the admiring faces of the crowd. A tender hand reached out to grip the boy's arm.

"We shall have a feast." she declared. The announcement inspired cheers from the onlookers. Four men grabbed the sled from the smiling hunter as his prideful mother and aunt hugged him grandly.

Ugidahli Unega was left alone at his aunt's house as his mother and aunt prepared for the evening's celebration at the dance field. He wondered what his uncle had told his mother about that morning. He remembered the look on his uncle's face as he watched him arrogantly cut the elk's throat in triumph. He had assumed anger, but as he reviewed it in his mind, perhaps it was more humiliation?

The door cover was drawn back and the remorseful boy looked up to see his uncle step inside. Ugidahli stood and faced his stoic uncle anxiously. His uncle glared at him with a cold, unemotional stare. He glared back and tried to show no emotion himself. It was as if his uncle had turned to stone and would never blink or move again. He could not match his uncle; it was more than he could bear.

"I want to hunt alone now," he stammered

Still, his uncle did not blink. He began to sweat and fidget with his fingers. At last, he detected a slight moistness in his uncle's eyes. His uncle announced bitterly.

"You do not hunt WITH me. I have no more to teach you."

With that, his uncle pivoted and exited the house.

CHAPTER

13

AN IMPROMPTU CELEBRATION ENSUED that night on the dance field. Ugidahli Unega felt that the weight of the world had been lifted from his shoulders. He felt liberated. For the first time in his life, he felt confident and self-assured. He was a man now. He no longer had to answer to anyone.

The vindicated hunter strutted through the congregating revelers and made his way to his busy mother. She immediately noticed the change in her son and stopped to study him. He arrogantly stood before her tall with chin up. She brushed his arm with her hand, looked him up and down, attempted a strained smile and then returned to her cooking. Turning, he looked down on his aunt, trying out his new attitude on her. At first, she seemed to not notice him, but then appeared to sense his presence and looked up at him. She smiled indifferently, then sliced a piece of meat and handed it to her nephew. She, too, became indifferent and returned to her work.

Unabashed, he journeyed on to the edge of the dance circle. *Perhaps I will dance tonight,* he ventured. He felt as though he could do anything he pleased. He was an adult. Haughtily he turned … there she was. She stared at him serenely, calmly, placidly. His stomach quaked; his face burned; but he stood steadfast. Now he had the confidence to approach her. Now was his time.

His legs responded to his command and he advanced toward her. But as he drew near the girl he had come to idolize, a tall, muscular boy passed in front of him and handed her a sliver of smoking elk meat. She smiled adoringly at the boy and accepted his gift graciously. Ugidahli now realized that her eyes had been upon this intruder all the while. The happy couple departed hand-in-hand leaving the unsettled hunter alone and dejected.

Infuriated, the rejected suitor threw his sliver of meat to the ground, stormed out of the village and headed for the waterfall. The thought of her having someone else had never occurred to him. She was HIS. When he reached the pond in front of the waterfall, he kicked off his moccasins and dove into the icy waters angrily.

The frigid waters took his breath away at first, but he stubbornly persisted, swimming beneath the surface of the water toward the humming sound of the water pouring into the pond. As he neared the confluence of the falls and pond, the humming grew into a loud rumbling. He was sucked into the crashing current. Squirming beneath the force of the falls, his unsympathetic lungs screamed for air.

In a last ditch surge he pulled himself past the confluence and flailed his way to the surface gasping for air. Exhilarated, he lazily swam to the cove behind the falls, pulled himself up on a ledge and wiped the cold water from his eyes. The falling water created an artificial breeze whipping through the cove leaving him shivering and chilled. He rubbed his shoulders and arms swiping the water off.

Slowly, the chill faded as his body adjusted and his breathing normalized. He kicked his dangling legs captivated by the agitated water. The image of her taking that boy's hand and walking away stirred him to kick violently splashing the water and turning it into white foam. He tried to drown out the roar of the waterfall with his own disturbance. Rage still fed his fury until his legs began to ache and his lungs complained. He dropped onto his back and breathed heavily with arms outstretched. "Why?" he screamed.

He pounded his fists on the floor of the rocky cove. He hated his life. He hated his uncle. His mother didn't really care about him. And now, the girl he was in love with was in love with someone else. The only people who cared about him were the old couple; the Kuni-Akati's.

… Well, that wasn't completely true. His grandmother, his father's mother, loved him. Maybe he could go to live with her. That would show them.

No, that probably wouldn't work. His grandmother would make him return. She wouldn't let him shirk his responsibility to provide for his mother in his father's absence.

But, if the old couple, Adawehi and Ajilusgi would take him in, no one would ever find him. That was it. That is what he had to do. He had to figure out how to get them to take him in.

Ugidahli Unega wallowed in self-pity in the cove behind the waterfall until dreams replaced his sorrowful thoughts and schemes. Something startled him. He lay still, blinking to clear his sleepy eyes. His ears perked to discern any sound outside the roar of the waterfall. Yes, he heard something random and not rhythmic like the pulsing water. Could it be voices? He sat up abruptly and listened closer. He tried to peer through the shining water, but the moonshine made it opaque.

He heard someone cackling. It was a girl, he thought. He crawled to his left so that he could look around the edge of the falling water. The voices became clearer. It was definitely a boy and a girl, but the angle of the moon prevented him from seeing more than shadowy figures sitting on the flat boulder where he had watched the nude bathing in the light of the full moon. The moon had been higher then, now the quarter moon was barely above the tree line.

The spy slid quietly off the cove ledge into the water and quietly paddled to the edge of the pond where two rounded boulders hid him from the couple. The girl spoke.

"Are you sure that was not you spying on me the other night?"

"Would I have run off like a scared rabbit?"

"Maybe, if you were trying not to get caught."

The boy laughed haughtily, "I do not sneak around."

The girl persisted, "It sure looked like you."

"It wasn't me." the boy retorted angrily.

There was silence for a moment before the girl continued, "I wonder who it could've been?"

After a pause, the boy offered, "Maybe it was your forest imp."

Ugidahli Unega heard a slapping sound. He carefully peered around the boulders. He was startled by how close he was. Patches of his eidelon's pretty face gleamed amidst the dark shadows of the overhanging trees. The boy was mostly illuminated from the waist up.

"Ouch." the boy feigned as he rubbed his shoulder. "Why'd you do that?"

"There is nothing wrong with the forest people."

"Yeah, but he's strange."

"What do you mean? You don't even know him."

"Well, his dad was sure strange."

"You knew his father?"

"My father talked about him. Father said he stayed to himself and never associated with his clan brothers. Nobody liked him."

The pretty girl frowned and turned to her brash boyfriend, "Why?"

"He was just a big old bruiser; always sullen and angry."

"Maybe they were afraid of him."

The boy shook his head and chuckled. "Well … maybe. He was what his name implied—a big old bear."

"Careful. You'll call back his spirit."

"I didn't say his name exactly."

The couple looked about trying to appear nonchalant. Ugidahli let his head rock back against the round boulders. It was strange to hear another point of view about his father.

"So, the big old bear was Bear Clan?"

"Yeah."

"What clan is his son?"

The boy wiped his face with his hand and pinched his chin, "Hmmm. I think his mother is Deer Clan."

"Which explains how he downed that big elk with one arrow."

The boy shrugged. "Not really. Father said that the boy's uncles hated his father so much they wouldn't have anything to do with his son until after his father died."

As the moon advanced across the sky dome, more of the girl's face became illuminated. The moon glow gave her dark, lovely face a silvery sheen. She put her hands flat on the stone beside her and rocked forward, "He must be a fast learner."

The boy's face was now halfway shaded. He squirmed a bit, "Maybe he picked up some stuff from his father. He was supposed to be a pretty good hunter in his own right."

The girl smiled mischievously and turned to look challengingly into the boy's eyes. The boy squirmed more, "What?"

The challenger giggled and turned away kicking her legs out and back. The boy shoved her forward and she laughed playfully. The boy reached out to push her again, but she dodged and he fell forward. The girl giggled triumphantly and sprinted into the dark forest with the boy racing after her.

Ugidahli pivoted around to catch a glimpse of the couple disappearing into the bushes and then turned back to lean against the cold boulders. He was shivering from squatting in the cold water for so long. He kicked out his feet and let himself float down to sit on the bottom of the pond. The water temporarily felt warm on his shoulders as his chin rested on the surface of the rippling waters. He lowered his chin and blew into the water in frustration.

"Well, she's not a spirit." he consoled himself. The couples' conversation rolled through his mind. *Forest IMP. Is that what I am?*

Then he smiled. "He must be a fast learner," she had said.

His tremors returned. He lifted himself out of the pond. The weight of his buckskin shirt sagged on his shoulders and stuck to his chest and stomach. He pulled the cold shirt away from his skin. The breeze was only slight, but enough to make his skin feel icy. He crossed his arms and sloshed through the grass to the infamous flat stone.

"You heard everything, didn't you?"

The soaked boy spun around. The figure of the girl gave off a bluish hue in the moonshine. Ugidahli searched for her companion. She giggled, "It's ok. I ditched him."

The illusive girl strolled confidently over to the drenched, shivering spy. She sat next to him, "So?"

Ugidahli was at a loss for words. She explained, "Were you the one spying on me here the other night?"

He wanted to flee, just as he had done that night, but his confident side challenged him to stay and face up to her, "Yes," he managed.

The beautiful inquisitor's eyes sparkled, "Why did you run away?"

"I dunno," he mumbled.

The sound of her laugh made his heart soar. It was the most endearing sound he had ever heard. "I saw you watching me pick strawberries."

His face felt hot. "I … uh … was waiting for my father … the search party to return."

The lovely girl turned her dark, tender eyes on him and smiled consolingly as she placed her hand on his wrist. Her face contorted and she withdrew her hand spreading her fingers and holding them up to her crossed eyes. Her nose wrinkled, "Ew."

Ugidahli burst into laughter. It felt good. She wiped her wet hand on her dress and giggled giddily.

For a wonderful moment, the couple laughed together and then sat together silently. At last, he had actually connected with her. She had actually spoken to him.

Without looking at him, she asked, "Do you have a name, forest person?"

He laughed again, "I am Ugidahli Unega … Ani Kawi."

"Tlvdatsi Sakonige, Ani Gilohi Clan."

"White Feather" looked at "Blue Panther" curiously. Although he had never met anyone of the "Twister" or "Long Hair" clan, he had heard that they thought of themselves as superior to everyone else.

"Hmm," he said as he turned back to stare at the pond thoughtfully.

The girl wrinkled her brow, leaned forward and attempted to look into his eyes as if searching for an explanation for "Hmm."

"What do you mean, hmm?" she challenged.

Devilishly, he grinned and shrugged, "Huh? Oh, … nothing."

The girl frowned and cocked her head to indicate she was not satisfied with his answer. But before she could challenge him further, her boyfriend's voice interrupted from a distance, "Sakonige, Tlvdatsi Sakonige."

Tlvdatsi Sakonige sighed and looked away. Ugidahli held his breath and waited to see if she would respond to her caller or stay with him and avoid the intruder.

She made her decision, placed her hand on his wrist again, "I guess I'd better go. He won't like it if he sees you here with me."

With that, she dashed off into the darkness. In the distance, he heard her shouting musically, tauntingly to his rival, "Udelehi. Udelehi Gahlida."

What have I done? What have I said? I am surely doomed. The clan will punish me for what I have said.

U GIDAHLI UNEGA WAS AWAKENED by a splashing sound and he could hear clicking sounds to his left. He lay still and struggled to open his eyes and let consciousness flow into him. Rotating his head toward the subtle clicks, he realized that he had slept on the flat stone by the falling water pond and the back of his head was sore.

It was a foggy morning and he felt wet. A cloud of soupy fog drifted past him obscuring the pond and falls. Then a visage materialized as the fog passed. The waking boy rose up on one elbow and studied the curious figure of an old man, almost naked with a single white feather angling up from behind a leather headband.

The old man's mouth was moving as he dipped his right hand into the water, raised the dripping hand up to the sky, muttering some indiscernible chant, then splashed the remainder of the water on his face and rubbed the runoff on his bare chest. He opened his other hand to reveal two shiny stones which he gently held down on the surface of the pond.

Ugidahli Unega listened curiously,

Gha. Tsane:hlanv:hi.

The boy recognized the old Uku who had taken them to water at his father's funeral. He was calling on the "provider" to "make his stones alive."

The old man continued, "You have just come to raise me up. I have just come to ask you things."

The old priest glanced about him as if making sure he was alone. He was startled to see the boy lying on the stone. He glared at the boy as he slowly stood and approached the observer.

"Who are you?" the priest commanded.

Ugidahli jumped to his feet respectfully, "Forgive me, Grandfather, I am Ugidahli Unega, Ani Kawi, my mother is Awi Ganvnvi."

The high priest's eyes softened as he drew back his head slightly looking down on the boy, studying his face. "Why are you spying on me, Ugidahli Unega?"

"Oh … uh … uh …" he stammered, "I … uh … wasn't spying, Grandfather."

The high priest frowned and turned his head slightly as if questioning the boy's answer. He quickly explained, "I fell asleep on the flat rock and just awoke when I heard you chanting."

The Uku raised his eyebrows, but continued to study the boy. The boy continued, "I will leave now, Grandfather."

As the rattled boy turned, the Uku interrupted, "Stay."

The fleeing boy froze.

The old Uku's face softened again changing to a kindly demeanor, "Sit with me."

The Uku sat beside the boy on the flat boulder. "Why do you not sleep at home with your grieving mother?"

The shy boy shrugged. The old man studied the sad boy. He made Ugidahli uncomfortable. Ukus were connected to the spirit world and could look into one's soul. The Uku whispered, "You miss your father?"

Again Ugidahli shrugged. He didn't know how to respond. The wizard continued to study him. "Do you have any questions for me?"

The bashful boy looked up at the kindly Elder. This was his chance. "Are you a Kuni-Akati?"

The Uku was at first taken back by the question, then amused. "No. A Kuni-Akati is for warriors. I am for all the people. I am an Uku."

Ugidahli turned away disappointed. The Uku questioned, "Why do you ask?"

The boy shrugged again, so the Uku persisted, "Do you know a Kuni-Akati?"

Ugidahli remembered his promise to the old couple. He reached up and touched the necklace he kept hidden under his shirt unconsciously. The priest studied the gesture as the boy shrugged.

"We have no Kuni-Akatis in the village anymore. If we were to go to war, we would have to rely on someone from another village to help our wounded. If you know of a Kuni-Akati somewhere, I would like to meet him."

The boy looked up at the Uku excitedly, but then remembered his promise. He turned away and then he shrugged.

The two sat quietly in thought until the boy changed the subject, "What are you doing with the stones?"

The old Uku chuckled, looked down and opened his hand to reveal the stones, "I am restoring life to the stones so that I can use them for divining."

Ugidahli was confused. "Divining?"

The Uku continued to stare at the stones, "When the stones are alive, they are connected to the spirit world and I can call upon them to give me the truth."

The student studied the stones, "How?"

The old man chuckled, "Well, suppose that you think that someone has put the sickness under you, but you're not sure. I could ask the stones and they would tell me whether you are cursed or ok."

"Like the bird meat?"

The Uku looked puzzled, then turned his eyes into space as if remembering the ceremony he performed for the boy after the funeral to determine if he would live a long life after his father's death. His eyes flared as if remembering something surprising. Ugidahli recognized the expression as the same one the Uku had expressed when the bird meat had flashed and sparkled without popping. It was a strange occurrence that the Uku said he had never seen before. The Uku turned to study Ugidahli. "I will finish the conjure to breathe life into the stones and then show you how it works."

Ugidahli's eyes lit up. The Uku placed his hand on the boy's knee, "You stay here while I finish the conjure."

The old Uku rose and trudged back to the pond where he kneeled and dipped his hand into the waters. He once again called upon the Provider to bring his stones to life. After repeating the conjure four times, the Uku stood and motioned for the boy to join him. They waded into the pond where the high priest put a stone in each hand and placed his thumbs over them. He closed his eyes and muttered a new conjure:

Une:hlanv:hi glavla?di tsa:hlido:hi:sdi hna:gwo da:sgino:hiseli. Nu:sdv gada:nv:dhe:sgv:I agwadu: liha agwade:logehisdi:I duyg:ghodvi.

The eloquent conjure sounded poetic and magical to the boy. The Uku's eyes were closed and he appeared to be feeling the stones. Ugidahli studied the stones curiously. Suddenly, the priest's eyes opened wide. He stared at the boy with a fierceness that made him very nervous.

"What is it?" he cried.

"But, you are of the Ani Kawi, are you not?"

"Yes, Grandfather, I am of the Deer Clan."

The Uku closed his eyes again and repeated the conjure. The nervous boy was beginning to get worried. What were the stones telling the Uku? Why was he asking again? Did the stones tell the Uku about his Kuni-Akati friends? Was it revealing his disrespect to his uncle? Could the Uku "see" him ogling the nude girl standing where they were now standing?

Again, the Uku opened his eyes and stared ominously at the boy. "The stones have told me that you possess a powerful connection with the spirits. Not only the deer and animal spirits, but plants and the spirits that look over human beings. Not natural for someone of the Ani Kawi. If you were Ani Gilohi or Ani Wodi, I would say you might make a fine medicine man."

The Uku laughed heartily at his private joke. "The deer are privileged to have you as their keeper."

Ugidahli was furious. "But, why can't I be a medicine man? What if I want to be a medicine man like … like you. What if I want to speak to the spirit world like you?"

Now embarrassed as well as angry, the boy crashed out of the stream and ran blindly into the forest with tears streaming from his eyes. When far enough away, he collapsed to his knees and cried, *What have I done? What have I said? I am surely doomed. The clan will punish me for what I have said.*

He wiped the tears from his eyes and sat back on his heels wondering what he should do next. Perhaps he should return to the Uku and plead for forgiveness; perhaps he should run into the forest and hide; maybe he could return to the old couple and hope they would take him in— maybe teach him to be a Kuni-Akati.

He heard russling behind him and turned to see the Uku. "Young Ugidahli Unega, it is normal to covet that which we are not; to seek to be that which is different and that we perceive as exciting. But what we learn when we reach the seventh level is that what we ARE is special too. That we should appreciate the talents we are given and be thankful and develop those talents to their potential. Therein we find happiness; therein we find harmony and peace. No one else possesses the talents you have and in the circle of life, you are special and crucial to your clan's role. Cherish that which you have been given."

"Yes, Uku." The boy hung his head sadly as the Uku touched his shoulder.

The Uku then patted his shoulder as he continued to speak. "Go to your grieving mother. You will find your happiness by making others happy. It is the Right Way, the White Way, the Tsalagi Way."

He had survived the fall. But, now, he was in danger of drowning in that merciful river that had rescued him.

Ugidahli Unega could not get the old couple and their medicines out of his mind. The idea of extracting the healing qualities of plants and using them to cure the curses devised by the animals seemed magical and exciting. The smells and images of the pots of medicine and animal parts in the strange seven-sided house of Adawehi and Ajilusgi flashed into his head as he dragged himself home. But, this magical world was not for him. He was bound to the dull life of the Ani Kawi.

His drying shirt was stiffening in the heat of the rising sun and irritating his skin. As he approached his house, he pulled the shirt over his head and brushed back the door cover to enter. He found his mother sitting alone by the hearth blankly stirring the glowing embers. He paused only momentarily before deciding not to disturb her. He strolled to his bed and tossed the stiff shirt on the floor as he dropped onto the bed forlorn.

"What is that?" his mother shrieked.

The startled son sat up quickly and searched the room desperately. His mother stood and charged at him with fire in her eyes, pointing her crooked finger at his chest. "Where did you get that?"

Ugidahli looked down at the sparkling necklace dangling from his neck. He reflexively covered it with his hands and turned his pleading eyes back to his mother's angry face.

"Ugidahli Unega. You have brought shame to your family. You must return that immediately."

Ugidahli Unega's mind was spinning. "It was a gift." he blurted out, but then caught himself. He had promised to keep the old couple a secret. What could he say to his furious mother? How could he explain?

"You accepted that which you have not earned? That which has no meaning for you? That which does not represent you? Now, Ugidahli Unega, return what you have purloined. Wear not that which bears your shame."

She could not continue as she collapsed to her knees overcome with screeching wails of despair, her crooked finger pointing to the door.

The horrified boy fled from the ignominious quagmire his mother has presented him, and ran madly into the welcoming folds of the forest where placid natural forces restore reason, harmony and balance to all things … in time. He was vanquished into this crux in his life, devoid of his senses, vexed and confused, blindly pushed by his exigent need for acceptance, fulfillment, purpose, and love. He ran on, and on, deep into the darkness and obscurity of the forest; a precious, welcoming oblivion.

The vanquished hunter, son, boyfriend, Kuni-Akati wannabe ran through the damp, pungent forest without direction or purpose; he just ran. His course was influenced by whatever opening presented itself; whatever path appeared before him; racing over knolls; crashing through streams; jumping over fallen tree trunks, driven by adrenalin from rage; devoid of plan or reason or consciousness.

As he topped the ridge and bounded over the boulder exposed by erosion, his legs continued to race and his arms wind milled as he vaulted into bounteous nothingness. As his momentum waned and he began the arcing descent into the vacuous canyon below, his breath was sucked out of his lungs and he felt the stinging thrill of his ever accelerating fall. Hyper-thought incited by his cataclysmic circumstance made his descent seem like slow motion by contrast.

He felt every cell in his body and every wind current that swirled through the canyon whipping him around leaving him helpless to correct his uncontrolled plunge to certain death. He felt his body rotating to a prone position facing the clouds above and imagined splattering on the canyon floor. But his flight continued and his body continued to rotate until he was looking up at his trailing feet and imagined cracking his skull on the boulders most certainly awaiting him below.

Frantically, he flapped his arms in a desperate effort to turn himself upright and just as the effort seemed to be working, he landed on his buttocks with a force that felt like his back snapped in two and his head whipped off his neck. Engulfed by darkness, his consciousness was overwhelmed by his hyper-mind going through its checklist examining his condition and circumstance. The process was interrupted by an immediate need for oxygen and the realization that he was being swept along by the swift current of the life-saving river.

He had survived the fall. But, now, he was in danger of drowning in that merciful river that had rescued him. Instinctively, he kicked and thrashed about until he reached the surface, gasping for relief. Water and air in equal measure, it seemed, filled his lungs as he was pulled under again briefly before resurfacing and allowing him to cough and fight for more air. Surface, cough, gasp, submerge; surface, cough, gasp, submerge. The all-powerful river current swept him relentlessly along, unsympathetic to his desperate fight to survive.

Gradually the raging river was calming, the undercurrents subsiding and his surfacing episodes were lasting longer, enabling him to catch glimpses of the river bank gliding past. Now he was flowing steadily along with his head above water and able to steer himself toward the bank a distance away. He was alright! His legs were working to keep him up, so his back was not broken, just sore. His neck was attached but stiff and aching from hitting the water. He ventured a look ahead to find the river appearing ever more calm as it curved toward the looming, thick forest ahead.

He would never know whether fate or his subconscious compass had intervened, but his journey had somehow led him to a familiar area.

A strong grip on his arm halted his passing and lifted him from the folds of the river! It belonged to a familiar, welcome face, his uncle, his father's brother.

The peaceful, contented uncle he had spent the lazy afternoon helping, startled his nephew with a loud yelp, jumped to his feet and began dancing enthusiastically around the fire pit.

GRANDMOTHER'S HOUSE WAS A small, one-roomed house nestled in a clearing surrounded by thick forest. It seemed uncannily familiar to Ugidahli. The smell of bread and cornmeal mixed with the powdery smell of packed dirt and dry bark reminded him of his house—the house where he grew up. The structure of the house was so similar to his old house. The way the roof beams were tied with the same knot his father used; the way the corner posts were notched so that the cross-beams fit exactly; the willow branches lined up so perfectly across the roof beams. He felt comfortable in this house.

The warmth of the crackling fire in the hearth damped the violent shivers of Ugidahli's cold but now dry body as he enjoyed the loving attention of his enormous grandmother, prodigious not only in size but also in generosity, kindness, and tenderness. As her loving hands blotted away the cold, dripping water from his hair with a soft cloth, the lucky boy felt the warmth of love he had rarely experienced in his lonely, independent life. Under the same circumstances, his father would have ignored him and his mother would have, at best, handed him the cloth to dry himself while chastising him for his careless, irresponsible behavior. But his capacious grandmother was tender and non-judgmental. He felt loved.

Ugidahli observed that his father's family's quiet, solemn ways were very different from his mother's family's boisterous arrogance. His father's family went about their day with almost no conversation, but there was a sense that they were very much in touch with each other. They helped each other without request. They did their individual thing without explanation or excuse. It was a comfortable, peaceful, respectful coexistence that Ugidahli admired and desired, but found difficult to adjust to. He was uncertain of how to fit in but eager to find his niche. He recognized this as the root of his father's quiet independence. It was not cold aloofness as he had supposed, but a confident assumption that love was present without need of expression.

Once dried, warm, and rejuvenated, the happy boy ventured outside where one of his uncles was sitting cross-legged in the porch shade wrapping flint-napped arrow heads onto raw, dried cane stalks. The hulking frame, skilled hands, quiet, contented demeanor was so reminiscent of his father. His uncle looked up at the curious boy and nodded for him to sit beside him. When he obliged, the younger version of his father handed him an arrowhead, twine, and nodded to the stack of cane stalks. Ugidahli was at first shocked and confused, but then realized that he was being invited to help. It made him proud and accepted.

Occasional dispassionate coaching constituted the whole of communication as the afternoon waned and Sister Sun headed for her home at the end of the sky vault. Despite the opportunity for contentment, the tormented boy's mind wandered freely from agonizing event to vexing predicament to infuriating encounter. Haunting memories stoking the fires of rage in his heart, rage that he yearned to share with his kindly uncle. But that would require verbal communication which seemed out-of-place at the moment.

As his uncle picked up the last cane stalk, Ugidahli's other uncles, equally large, lumbered into the clearing surrounding the humble, modest house. The oldest carried the carcass of a field-dressed deer draped around his broad, bulging shoulders. His grandmother appeared through the door and wiped her big meaty hands on her sack-like dress. The other three uncles dumped their armloads of firewood beside the blackened circular pit in the center of the clearing in front of the house and then started a fire.

The oldest uncle and his grandmother busied themselves mounting the graying, red meat on a long spit and hefted it into the "Y" segments of large tree branches mounted on either side of the fire pit. There would be a feast tonight.

Ugidahli forced himself to stuff one last piece of venison into his mouth and then leaned back against the porch post. The sweet smell of smoked deer meat now smelled sickening. He had eaten too much. Grandmother's bulging stomach grumbled as she belched loudly. Rubbing her full stomach, she smiled proudly at her visiting grandson. "There is more, grandson, eat your fill."

The stuffed boy gave a generous belch, blowing out his fat cheeks like a chipmunk, causing the family to laugh at his perfect response.

Uncle Ahuli, whose name means drum, appropriately produced a hollow stump covered by a stretched deer-skin and began to pound on it with a rabbit-skin tipped stick. It was the battered and scarred drum that Ugidahli had once crawled on top of as a child. The oldest uncle, the one called Ugowe, closed his eyes as if going into a trance and began chanting an old song. The youngest uncle's name was a mystery to Ugidahli. All he had ever heard him called was simply "Brother," or "Udo," as if, after five children, his grandmother had run out of names.

The peaceful, contented uncle he had spent the lazy afternoon helping, startled his nephew with a loud yelp, jumped to his feet and began dancing enthusiastically around the fire pit. His other two brothers yelped and stood deliberately and regally, and began their more restrained and sophisticated version of the dance. Ugidahli giggled joyfully at the impromptu spontaneity and lack of pretense. His mother's family would never behave so freely and immodestly.

Grabbing his hand, his grandmother pulled him into the dance. He was, at first, embarrassed and reluctant, but after some playful goading by his grandmother and Udo, he began to try to imitate his exuberant uncle by stomping and kicking and ducking, spinning awkwardly and clumsily around the blazing fire. It was fun; pure fun; something completely unfamiliar.

Cozily wrapped in the warm, comfortable bear skin, muffled voices drew the sleeping boy's attention. Pulling the blanket from his head, the bright morning sunlight and brisk cool air slapped his face and left him blinking and revived. The voices were coming from outside and he recognized the muffled tone of his grandmother speaking sternly. Rubbing his eyes, he pulled the blanket back over his head to return to the blissful slumber he was enjoying before the disturbance from outside. But it was not to be. The voices had piqued his curiosity.

He pulled back the blanket again and listened intently. He sensed that Grandmother was explaining something very important. Udo responded in a conciliatory tone ending the conversation. Pretending to sleep, the boy quickly buried his head in the blanket as his grandmother entered the room. "Rise now, Grandson. Sister Sun is searching for you."

Promptly he threw off the heavy bear blanket and stretched his stiff, sore muscles. Sitting up dutifully, he accepted a bowl of corn mush from his grandmother. She knelt down on her knees, sat back on her heels and patiently waited as her grandson wolfed down the soup. "Udo will accompany you home."

The boy looked up from the bowl and wiped gruel from his chin. His sad, pleading eyes studied his grandmother for a moment before appealing to her, "Can't I stay for a while?"

Her stern eyes softened sympathetically, "Your mother needs you and will miss you. You must go now."

With that, she rose purposefully and strode to the hearth, shouting toward the door, "Udo."

Uncle Udo entered the house carrying two bulky packs. "Ready to go, Little Deer?"

"Little Deer" stood sadly, took a deep breath, and straightened himself with new found pride. He had expected this to happen, but had hoped it wouldn't—not for a while anyway. This abrupt return to reality made him realize that for a moment, he had been a boy again. Returning would vault him back into the pseudo manhood he had fought for. He straightened, "I can find my way, Udo."

The prideful but heartbroken young man tugged at the pack. Udo glanced at his mother—Ugi's Grandmother—for affirmation. She nodded, and Udo released the pack smiling amiably at his nephew. "Want some company along your path?"

"No thanks, Udo."

CHAPTER

17

He felt a tingling in his right hand. He jumped back in astonishment releasing the stones. The stone had moved. He had felt the stone actually move. It was only slight, but it had definitely moved. The spirit was clearly directing him to take the path to the right.

IT WASN'T REALLY A lie. He would never lie, especially not to his Grandmother. Not because clan law required a liar to be put to death, but because his father had often taught him that a man's word is his soul. That to speak is a privilege and that words should have meaning and hold truth. Ugidahli was confident that he could "find" his way home merely by reversing his course and following the path that had led him to this place.

But, of course, he had no intention of going home. His plan was to retrace his path until he came to familiar territory and then find the old couple's curious, seven-sided house. He unconsciously touched the heavy necklace hanging on his bare chest and rubbed his hand across the beads and bear claws and round, netted crystal pocket. He would have to give the beautiful jeweled necklace back, but it would be worth it if Adawehi and Ajilusgi would take him in.

It was mid-morning before he reached the summit where he had taken the almost fatal step. He cautiously peered over the edge into the deep canyon. The rushing water below gave off a low, rumbling roar. In his mind, based upon how long he fell, the canyon should be much, much deeper. By contrast, the distance from where he entered the river to where he was plucked from the water by his uncle Ahuli was much, much farther than he imagined.

He took a deep sigh, relieved that such a cavalier action had not resulted in his death. He turned to continue his journey. But after only a short distance, he was confronted with a fork in the path. Which one had he come on? Should he go left or right? He really didn't know which path to take. As he studied his options and tried to find something familiar deep along either path, he had an epiphany—the stones!

He fingered the necklace. Couched in a circular cache with netting was a crystal smaller than his fist, made up of three crystal facets merged together. Dangling from the circular frame were two shiny, egg-shaped agate stones, one white and one black. A hole had been drilled in the tops and leather straps tied them to the base of the netted circle holding the crystal.

The two stones dangling at the bottom of his necklace were exactly what he needed. He must go back to the river and bring them to life with the sacred conjure he had heard the village Uku recite at the pond in front of the waterfall. With the stones, he could reach out to the spirits to tell him which path to take. The excited new student of conjuring turned and raced back to the river.

Quickly, Ugidahli Unega found a shallow, calm cove jutting into the bank of the river. He kicked off his moccasins and pushed off his pants. He waded into the shallow jetty and cupped water in his right hand as he began the conjure he had heard the old Uku recite. "Gha. Tsane:hlanv:hi."

He held his dripping hand up to the sky and continued, "Ha. Now you who can make the stones alive. You have just come to raise me up."

He then splashed the water on his face and rubbed the runoff on his bare chest. He cupped the two shiny stones dangling from his necklace in his hand and gently held them down on the surface of the pond. "I have just come to ask You things."

The apprehensive impersonator looked around nervously before continuing, "Now. Listen. Your soul has just been pushed against the middle Pathway where it divides."

The astute conjurer dipped his right hand into the water again and offered the water to the "Provider" as he began the second round of the conjure, "Gha. Tsane:hlanv:hi."

Ugidahli was unaware of his singularly great memory. He had lived away from other children growing up so he didn't know that total recall was unusual or rare. To him it was normal and simply available anytime he needed it. Had he even thought about it, he would surely have concluded that precise and complete memory was common and a talent possessed by all. But, connecting to the spirit world was new to him. He had never even suspected that he had this talent until the Uku had surprised him with the news. He wasn't sure what it meant to connect with spirits; what it would feel like; or how he would know when or if it happened. For now, he just trusted that with the aid of the stones and the water ceremony, it would happen.

It was during the third round of the conjure, while facing west, when he bent over to place the two stones on the surface of the water, that Sister Sun's fingers of light reached through the crystals in his dangling necklace and cast a glittering rainbow on the surface of the water in front of him. As he hushed his words to admire the sparkling spectacle, he noticed the image of a face in the midst of the rainbow. "Uncle Udo?" he whispered.

As the image became clearer to him, he could see that his uncle was hiding behind a large Maple tree. He looked up to the bank where the reflected Maple grew on a knoll near the bank of the river. A silhouette pulled back behind the tree. His uncle had followed him.

Angry, his first impulse was to shout at his covert uncle—to call him out. "Grandmother doesn't trust me!" he muttered to himself.

But, he loved his uncle. Udo and his Aunt Awinita seemed to be the only ones who understood him and accepted him. He was certain that poor Udo was just following orders. Even if he wasn't, he believed that Udo had good intentions and was just looking out for him. Ugidahli decided to act as if he didn't know his uncle was there. He smiled to himself and continued the conjure.

Having his uncle spy on him was awkward and irritating, but Ugidahli knew that confronting his uncle would not discourage him, just make him be more discrete. Maybe by not letting on that he knew he was following him, he could more easily keep track of him. Determined to proceed with his plan, he ignored his Uncle Udo.

When he reached the ambivalent junction that had left him in a quandary before, it was time to test the stones. He wasn't sure whether the stones would work without standing in water, but if nothing happened, he would return to the river and question the spirits from there. He placed the white quartz stone in his right hand and the black quartz in his left, placed his thumbs lightly over each, closed his eyes and recited the conjure the Uku had used to divine truth from his stones.

"Une:hlanv:hi. Something to use a stone with. Your resting place is Above. Now, you will tell me what I am thinking about. I want to learn the truth. Show me the way."

He felt a tingling in his right hand. He jumped back in astonishment releasing the stones. The stone had moved. He had felt the stone actually move. It was only slight, but it had definitely moved. The spirit was clearly directing him to take the path to the right.

Ugidahli Unega yelped loudly imitating his rowdy uncle Udo and then imitating his uncle's jubilant dance around an imaginary fire pit. He had connected. The spirits had spoken to him; him, little nobody him; an Ani Kawi. He had called upon the spirit world and it had responded. The triumphant medicine man wannabe gripped his magical necklace and raced off down the right-directed path.

CHAPTER

18

WITH EACH STEP, THE shadowy forest became more and more familiar until Ugidahli reached another fork in the path. He didn't need the divining stones to tell him where these two paths led. To the right would lead him to his destination—the seven-sided hut of the Kuni-Akati couple he sought, Adawehi and Ajilusgi. The left path led home to his self-centered, repressive mother and her angry, condescending family. But for one very menacing development, his choice would have been very simple. Uncle Udo.

Although he had not seen nor heard his uncle since the pond beside the river, he could not be certain that his grandmother's spy was not still following him. An inviting log enticed the boy to sit and ponder his situation. In his mind, he had three options. He could ignore his uncle and the consequences and seek out the old couple straight-away. He looked down at the gift that Adawehi had given him in confidence. Leading Udo to the hut of Adawehi and Ajilusgi would betray that confidence.

He could try to devise a clever trick to lose his uncle and then secretly double-back to the old couple's hut. But, his uncle was very clever and much more adept in the forest than he was.

Or, he could go home. Satisfied he had made it back safely, Udo would return to report to his grandmother that he had made it safely home. Then it would be a simple matter of disappearing again. But this option had all kinds of distasteful elements such as having to face his mother and explaining where he had been. And then there's the necklace. It was the reason he was banished from home in the first place.

Frustrated, he reached up and grasped the divining stones. Perhaps the spirits could tell him if his uncle was still following him. He rubbed the smooth, shiny surfaces of the two stones with his thumbs. When he closed his eyes, the image of his uncle hiding behind a tree flashed into his head. He turned quickly in time to see his uncle duck back behind the tree.

Then, it hit him. There was a fourth option. Uncle Udo was probably unaware that his mother was now living in the village instead of in their remote home in the woods along the stream. That was it. He would simply return to the old home of his father and mother. Once Uncle Udo was satisfied and returned to give his report to Grandmother, he could resume his journey back to the old couple.

When the clever trickster reached his old home by the stream, a diabolical idea struck him. Instead of walking around the bend in the stream to the vacant house, he diverted to cross the stream instead. When he reached the middle of the stream, he held out his necklace to the sun. Then, discreetly, he turned to look at the rainbow in the stream made by the crystal. Sure enough, in the midst of the dancing colors was the reflected image of his uncle standing at the edge of the woods.

Nonchalantly, the clever diviner waded out of the stream and entered the house. Stealthily, he peered through the window to watch his uncle's reaction. His uncle appeared to be satisfied, turned and vanished into the woods.

Proud of himself, but still suspicious, he dropped his pack next to his bunk. He would spend the night before continuing on his journey. He did not want to overtake his uncle should his uncle decide to bed down for the night before returning home.

Out of habit, the boy turned to go sit by the hearth and the warmth of the fire that had always burned there. The ghostly image of his father sat in his usual spot by the hearth. His father turned his head slowly to look at his son before slowly fading. The startled son shrieked and jumped back. As the image faded, the skin and eyes dripped off leaving the skeletal face which slowly dissolved until only the unfamiliar tomb remained. Unnerved by the visage, he backed up slamming into his bunk and plopped down abruptly.

In a way, he wanted the ghost to return. In a way, he feared it would. The lonely boy lay down on the bed and focused on the slate stones capping the tomb containing the remains of his father. Watching, hoping, fearing he might get one more glimpse of his father, the nervous boy decided that he would retreat to the porch to sleep.

When the haunted teenager finally awoke the next morning, the sun was casting short shadows across the meandering stream beside the abandoned house. His arm was peppered with goose-flesh from the morning chill. The familiar vivid fragrances of the forest and stream comforted him—he was home. But the house smelled differently. It smelled old and stale. It was cold and un-inviting in its abandoned state.

He was surprised by how soundly he had slept. Sitting up quickly, rubbing his eyes and breathing deeply, he quickly glanced inside at the hearth checking for the ghost of his father. Only the tomb marked the spot.

He stretched grandly and then stood to return inside. Curious, he slipped over to the window and peeked out between the billowing window curtain and edge of the window. There was no sign of his nuisance of an uncle. He rubbed the agate stones and closed his eyes. No flashing images of his uncle.

Relieved and excited about his newfound freedom, he dug into the pack his grandmother had prepared for him for the last of the cornbread cakes. Chewing ravenously on the sweet cake, he threw his pack over his shoulder and headed to the river for a drink. His thirst hastily quenched, he checked out the rainbow created on the water by his dangling necklace. It was empty, he was safe. Ugidahli crashed through the stream alternating bites of the tasty, crumbling cake with handfuls of cold stream water.

The warming air and the frigid water were a refreshing introduction to his new freedom. He felt relieved of binding family ties; he felt empowered. Excited about his new found independence, he leaped from the stream and raced into the forest. At last he could pursue his all-consuming desire to go live with Adawehi and Ajilusgi and learn the tantalizing secrets of the Kuni-Akati.

There was a gleam in his eyes as he remembered the initial days but then the twinkle dwindled and died. "The dark world can be very dark indeed. No man can understand all of the traps of the dark world, and no man should try."

THE COMPOUND WHERE ADAWEHI and Ajilusgi lived was so different from the last time he saw it that at first he thought he was at the wrong place. The fertile fields of corn, beans, and squash were overgrown with dry, brittle weeds. The stilted corn storage building was listing and would soon fall. The low, rounded roof of the asi was barely visible behind the volunteer vegetation enshrouding it. There was no mistaking the unique house with its seven walls, but it was untended, with large sections of plaster missing from the walls. The pungent smells that had captured his imagination during his last visit were now replaced with the putrid stench of rotting death. There was, however, smoke rising from the vent in the top of the house.

The bewildered returning visitor waded through the overgrowth to the decaying porch where he stopped. *What had happened? How had the place come to this in so short a time?*

A raspy voice from the dark shadows inside the house interrupted his thoughts. "Why have you returned?"

The boy gasped, recoiled and then studied the darkness, waiting for his eyes to adjust. The ghostly silhouette of a decrepit old man stood inside the doorway. As his eyes adapted, he could see that the spent man was stooped and withered.

"Adawehi?" he offered doubtfully.

"Why have you returned?"

Undeterred, he rushed in to support the fragile old man, "What has happened to you?"

The old man pushed him away with a boney hand, "You must go away."

His eyes darted about the dark room, "Where is Ajilusgi?"

From a dark corner a frail, sickly voice cried out, "Who is there?"

Ugidahli felt the boney hand again, "Go away before she sees you. You must leave and never look back."

Determined, he grasped the fragile arms of the old man, "I will not leave. Tell me what has happened."

Sad, tearing, red eyes looked up at the determined visitor and relented. Ugidahli followed the old man into the sweltering heat of the house to the hearth where a full fire crackled.

Resignedly, Adawehi explained, "Ugidahli Unega has returned."

The weak, desperate voice of Ajilusgi cried out, "He must leave."

Ugidahli rushed to the bedside of the old woman and knelt beside her, "What has happened?"

In a hateful, bitter voice she decried, "You have put this under us. You must go away and never think of us again."

He was confounded by her attack and left speechless listening to her heart wrenching sobs. He felt the spidery fingers of Adawehi clench his shoulder. "He cannot be blamed for what he does not understand."

The fleshy hand of the dying woman reached out. He clutched her hand with both of his. His mind was spinning. *How could this be his fault? He would not place anything under them.*

"Why did you come back, Grandson?"

Where should I start? "I have nowhere else to go, Grandmother."

He could read doubt and confusion in her tearful, reddened eyes. He tried to explain, "My father has gone to the upperworld. My mother grieves only for herself. My mother's uncles hate me. I cannot stay there anymore."

Adawehi removed his hand from the boy's shoulder and shuffled off to the hearth. The old woman squeezed the boy's hands and shook them as if she could shake loose her words into his hands but her emotions blocked her words. Ugidahli sympathetically gave her time.

After a moment, she garnered the strength to whisper, "Your grandmother loves you."

"I love you, too, Grandmother."

The old woman gasped and then snorted an endearing chortle that was enjoined by her husband. The reaction unsettled the sincere grandson.

"I mean your father's mother," she managed before being seized by giddy giggles that provoked an involuntary belly laugh from her husband. That then caused a wheezing seizure in the old woman.

As the paradigm shifted in his head and his faux pas glared at him, Ugidahli's laugh reflex was provoked as well and the three timorous friends enjoyed a rare moment of loving laughter.

Laughing felt good especially for the residents of the gloomy heptagonal house of mystery. Ugidahli sensed that his return had lifted their spirits despite their insistence that they had dreaded his return. Surely, they could now see that they not only wanted him to stay, they needed him in a psychological and physiological way. The long silence was getting awkward for the enthusiastic visitor. "You know my grandmother?"

This remark chilled the levity. The old woman's face transitioned into a sad, reminiscent state as her eyes turned to stare into the darkness above her. Adawehi held his breath in anticipation of her answer. Even the young boy could sense the tension that was building in her.

Ajilusgi sucked in a deep breath, "Yes, I know your grandmother. ... We were once very close."

Adawehi shifted nervously. He reached for his pipe as their visitor asked the obvious follow-up question, "What happened?"

Ajilusgi did not stir and he was not sure she heard the question, but he waited respectfully. Her eyes were dancing back and forth as if she were viewing some event unfolding before her. Adawehi decided to come to her defense. He started to rise, a difficult task, and his grunting and clumsy struggles drew the youthful listener over to assist him.

"Wado." He managed, "I think it is time that we walk."

They had no more left the house than the struggling Adawehi found a stump near the porch to sit. With closed eyes he gasped for air. Ugidahli was worried that even this small journey was too much for the stooped old man who seemed to be aging before his very eyes.

Finally, the old man ceased gasping, steadied himself and stared at the ground. "We have not been honest with you."

Ugidahli could not grasp what the old man was saying. He had never met anyone who had purposefully told a lie. He had been taught that your word is your soul and that anyone who would tell a lie would also be dishonest in their actions. He was told that liars were put to death so that their deceitful ways could venture no further.

"We are not Kuni-Akati," the sorrowful confessor raised his eyes to stare frankly into the eyes of his young friend, "We are Tsigili."

"Witches?" exclaimed his startled young friend.

The gaze of the witch returned shamefully to the ground. Ugidahli's mind was filled with a quagmire of conflicting emotions. Tsigili's were evil; they were to be feared and avoided.

The remorseful witch searched for a way to calm the hurricane of thought imploding in his young mind and to bring him back to safe ground.

"We are not malicious witches. But, we were seduced into the dark world by its mystical, magical, … tantalizing mysteries."

There was a gleam in the old man's eyes as he remembered the initial days but then the twinkle dwindled and died. "The dark world can be very dark indeed. No man can understand all of the traps of the dark world, and no man should try."

The harrowed witch shook his head sadly.

Rattled, Ugidahli was trying to follow but this was too much to absorb. What could be mystical, magical, or tantalizing about the dark world? He sat quietly, numb, not knowing how to respond. This man who had seemed so wonderful, now …?

The old man studied the now quiet, silent boy. He shook his head resignedly, "This is not what you expected. We are not what you thought."

The old man wearily rose and sadly turned to return inside. "Perhaps you should go home now."

… figuring out the tricks is one thing, being able to connect with the spirits is a special gift only few possess.

NUMBLY, UGIDAHLI STUMBLED DOWN the path to the stream. His head was spinning, *What just happened? That kind old man and loving old woman were not what tsigilis were supposed to be like. They weren't devious or evil or mad.*

He found himself standing by the stream. *Where to now?* Would his real grandmother take him back if he begged her? Could he swallow his pride and return to his mother and her family? Deep in thought, he fingered the necklace. *The necklace!*

He rushed back. He would have to return the necklace. He had broken his promise and, besides, he could not return home with the "purloined" necklace.

As he passed by the window, he heard voices. Adawehi stood beside his wife in the dark room holding her feeble hand. He could just see that she had been crying but was now resigned to hear the bad news.

Adawehi patted and then rubbed her hand, "He has gone home. It was too much for him."

She did not respond. A tear trickled down her cheek. Ugi could see that she loved her young intruder. A tear rolled down his cheek. She looked so withered and forlorn. Her stinging words echoed in his head, "You have put this under us. You must go away and never think of us again."

Light from outside flashed across the floor as he drew the door cover back. His shadow stretched into the room. "Your necklace," he stammered holding out the bulky necklace.

The stunned old couple did not move or respond.

"So, what is it that you suppose I put under you?"

Adawehi turned, "What?"

"You said that I put the thing under you. What did I put under you?"

Ajilusgi pushed Adawehi coaxing him to go to Ugidahli. The old wizard looked at his wife, turned, and shuffled to the fireplace, "Come sit with me."

Ugidahli joined the old man and draped the prized necklace on the hearth. "It is a magical necklace."

The old man studied the boy as he tamped tobacco into his pipe. "How so?" he questioned as he reached for a splint and lit it from the fire in the hearth.

Ugidahli laid a log on the fire. As the glow brightened, he could see the enthusiasm in the old man's eyes as he explained, "I brought the stones to life and they divine the truth when I ask. And the crystal shows me images in the water."

Smoke billowed up as Adawehi brought his pipe to life. "How did you 'bring the stones to life'?"

Proudly, Ugidahli stood and went through the motions to show the old man how he went to water. He dipped his hand into the imaginary pond and splashed it on his face and chest. He explained how he asked the provider to bring the stones to life and recited the conjure.

The wizard was impressed. He shook his head slowly in disbelief. "Where did you learn that conjure?"

Bursting with pride, Ugidahli sat down again and accepted the pipe from his captivated host, "I learned it from the Uku."

The conjurer beamed a smile as he drew on the old man's pipe. Too late, he remembered to be careful with the smoke, and he once again found his lungs filled and struggling to expel the unexpected burning intrusion. He remembered how Ajilusgi had coaxed him to relax and with some effort regained control. He cleared his throat several times, as he handed the pipe back to his host.

"And the crystal?"

He reluctantly took back the pipe, carefully inhaled a small draw on the pipe and slowly allowed the burning smoke to escape. He waited. With a small irritating cough, but nothing severe, he continued. "When I bent over in the pond, I just happened to notice the colors dancing on the water. As I watched them sparkle, I saw the image of my uncle spying on me from the bank."

He tried the pipe once more—this time more success-fully—before handing it back to Adawehi. The old man smiled proudly at the determined rookie smoker.

After enjoying the pipe himself for a while, the old man queried, "Why was your uncle spying on you?"

Eager to add to his success, the rookie smoker carefully inhaled a larger amount of smoke, held it, and then slowly released the irritating smoke, just as he had observed of Adawehi. This time the smoke warmed his lungs and tasted sweet as it passed out through his mouth. He held the pipe admiringly before him and said with a smirk, "This is very good isn't it?"

Adawehi smiled knowingly.

He tried the pipe successfully again. Now he felt as though he were mastering this token of manhood. As the last of the smoke left his mouth, he remembered that Adawehi had posed a question. "My uncle was making sure I went home, I guess."

After one more triumphant pass on the pipe, he directed the conversation back to his intrigued host. "So, what is the thing I put under you and how do we remove it?"

He could hear a slight snort from Ajilusgi as Adawehi accepted the pipe and smoked while he gathered his thoughts. At last, he continued, "We have followed the black path too long and dark spirits have poisoned our askinas."

Adawehi must have seen that 'askina' was an unfamiliar concept for the inexperienced young man. The old man looked down in thought, then looked into the young man's eyes. "Askina is your essence, what makes you who you are, your life's connection. It is your souls."

Adawehi enjoyed the pipe again and looked quizzically into the flames in the hearth. "We were in favor with the spirits of the underworld and they sustained and gave us health."

He paused as if remembering something sad. A trickle of smoke drifted up from the pipe as he held it across his lap. "The power that they gave us is a sacred trust not to be abused. If we carelessly expose ourselves to a … a 'seer', then we break that trust and the spirits take back that power."

Despondent, the old man turned his sad eyes to his young friend. "You do not know the connection that you have with the spirits. You are a seer. When you saw the 'sparkling ravens', you were seeing Ajilusgi and myself in our evil pretext; your powers of sight penetrated our disguise. You unwittingly stripped from us the spell the spirits had entrusted with us. The sickness that the spell concealed; the decomposition of aging that the dark magic allayed; the term of life extended by witchery; were all revoked leaving us naked and vulnerable to the afflictions of the flesh and the transience of life. The good health granted to us by the underworld was forfeited."

Before realizing his impertinence, Ugidahli blurted out, "Do you not have a medicine for yourself?"

The old man chuckled at his naiveté but then grew very stern. "We need more than medicine to heal us now."

"Tell me what you need and I will get it for you. Tell me what to do and I will do it for you," their impatient but passionate servant cried out to him desperately.

Adawehi looked at Ugi sadly. "If only you COULD help. Clearly, you have something very special. To discover the secrets of the necklace was an extraordinary achievement. Even experienced witches might not have put it together as quickly and effectively as you have. But, figuring out the tricks is one thing, being able to connect with the spirits is a special gift only few possess."

Adawehi shook his head, "You asked what you put under us. In truth, it is what you removed."

The boy's eyes became large and intense. He remembered the Uku saying that he was special and could connect with the spirits. He remembered the bird meat sparkling on the hearth. "If I have a special gift. If I can connect with the spirits as you say. Why can't I call upon the spirits to put it back?"

Adawehi appeared to be stunned by the question. His brow furrowed. He peered into the seer's eyes deeply. "Perhaps you can."

Ugidahli Unega's eyes burned red and sparks began to spew from his arms as his head began to change into the shape of the raven's head.

Ugidahli was up long before Sister Sun made her appearance. He had slipped out of the house quietly so as not to wake his snoring mentors. He should have been exhausted after pressing them for information so late into the night, but the more he learned, the more he wanted to learn! He never wanted to stop, but they had insisted after he had prodded them into explaining the contents of every bowl or pot full of plant and animal concoction including not only its use, but the related conjure, as well. He had drained them of their energy and they had collapsed moments after he released them from his constant interrogation. Even then, his mind had continued to race throughout the night, sorting, organizing and expanding on the munificent information garnered from the wizards. Inventive ideas sprouted prolifically and drove him into the night to search for fresh ingredients to test. By the time the morning light of Sister Sun came, his search was done and his basket was full. The thought of sharing his inventions with his wise and experienced counselors excited him.

Adawehi waited for the first light of morning to validate his rising. He was up early not because he was an early riser by nature, but because of his bladder. He had slipped out of the house quietly so as not to wake his loudly snoring wife nor his new apprentice, a lump under his blanket who had not even moved since he had awakened some time ago. *The boy must be exhausted after his voracious quest for information.*

Adawehi had been amazed by the boy's enthusiasm but absolutely astounded by his retention. He seemed able to retain every minute piece of information they presented him; he absorbed the knowledge like a dry sponge absorbs water. And he never wanted to stop.

As the old man approached the house, he was experiencing something he had not experienced for a long, long time—excitement. He was actually anxious to get the day started and to spend more time with his boy wonder. For the first time in many years, he felt needed and important. The unexpected visit had brought meaning back into his life. And he was also excited about the positive affect the boy was having on Ajilusgi.

He wanted to march into the house and roust the boy out of bed. He only had so much energy and the mornings were the best time for him. But, he also remembered how much young people were attached to sleep, particularly in the morning. He had been the same when he was young. So, he sat on the old stump he had placed in the shade of the porch to wait.

"Osiyo, Grandfather."

The greeting of the eager apprentice did not come from inside. The enthusiastic student came bounding up from the forest carrying a large clay bowl filled with plant samples.

"I have been gathering fresh plants to replace the rotting ones in your supply. Oh, and I want to try some things on you and Ajilusgi that I've been thinking about. They might make you feel better, at the very least."

Adawehi beamed brightly and grew a wide smile. This boy was fun; undeniably, genuinely, fun.

So began Ugidahli Unega's education and journey down the dark path of witchcraft. Within days, he had mastered the lexicon of plant medicines and conjures. His energy was unlimited and relentless. Adawehi did not have the strength to satisfy all the boy's insatiable questions. His strength was rapidly waning. But when he was forced to rest, Ugi was extracting information from Ajilusgi or trying some clever concoction and conjure he had invented. The boy was determined to find the secret to curing his dear friends.

Whether or not Ugidahli's creative concoctions were working, or the adrenaline generated by his excitement and eagerness was the cause, Adawehi and Ajilusgi were miraculously improving.

Working with Adawehi and Ajilusgi was, for Ugidahli, the happiest experience of his life. It reminded him of that lazy afternoon beside his uncle Udo. *This must be what mentoring should be like. These are the things a boy should learn from his uncles and the clan. This is how it could have been with my father's family.*

Sheltered from the cooling breeze of twilight next to the porch wall, Adawehi adeptly chopped off the head of the healthy, struggling raven as he explained to his attentive apprentice, "To be able to shape-shift into the visage of a raven, you must transfer his askinas, his souls, to yourself at the proper time and in the proper sequence."

Like a surgeon, he sliced open the trunk of the bird and extracted the heart, liver, and rib bone as he continued, "The first askina is the soul of physiological life and is captured by consuming the liver within seven days of death. Consuming the heart within one moon cycle captures the askina of circulation. And finally, consuming the marrow of the bone captures the askina of structure and shape."

The astute apprentice had learned that every potion, charm, or spell required a conjure, prayer, or imprecation to make it work. But he was surprised by how complex and eloquent the conjure was for transferring the raven's askinas, including many archaic words that had long since lost their definition.

After reciting the conjure and consuming the liver, heart, and bone marrow of the raven, Adawehi lead the witch-in-training to water. As they approached the stream, the teacher stopped and pointed to the Aholiyehvsgi plant growing beside the path.

"You will need the root of that plant."

The student obediently extracted the root. Adawehi instructed his student to wash the root in the flowing stream and say a prayer to make the juices of the root "the helper to bring things together." "Chew the root for the bitter juices. They will be a catalyst to meld the askinas of the raven with your askinas."

Adawehi began one of his trademark stories as they continued along the darkening path beside the river. "Long ago, eight young boys became so angry with their mothers that they prayed to the spirits to help them escape into the sky. The boys danced around the Council House until they lifted off the ground and began to float upwards. One of the mothers managed to pull her son down, but the others rose into the sky to join the spirit world. We will pray to the seven boys to share with us the power of flight."

The two confederates of witchcraft continued their walk alongside the river to a point where beaver dams blocked the flow of the stream and created a tranquil pond. The dark forest and bright spirit campfires in the sky reflected in the calm waters. Adawehi cautioned his apprentice to try not to disturb the waters as they waded into the pond.

The Aholiyehvsgi juice was already affecting the boy so he felt as if he could float above the waters. Once they were waist deep in the pond, Adawehi demonstrated for the novice, who copied his motions, spreading his arms overhead reaching into the darkening sky. They waited for the water to settle and then dropped their heads. Adawehi pointed out the seven stars of the Ani Tsutsa, the constellation of the seven boys, reflecting in the water directly in front of them.

Ceremonially, they brought down their arms circumscribing a circle terminated by scooping up the water containing the reflection of the Ani Tsutsa and splashing it on their foreheads and rubbing it over their faces and chests. Again, they raised their arms up to the Ani Tsutsa and called upon the boys to extend to them their powers of levitation.

Ugidahli Unega's eyes burned red and sparks began to spew from his arms as his head began to change into the shape of the raven's head. The shape-shifting apprentice's arms changed into black wings as he extended them level with his shoulders and shot into the sky. Fire and sparks streamed from his arms and body as the terrified young witch's shriek echoed through the surrounding forest. The slightest adjustment to his arms altered his flight dramatically. His heart was pounding out of his chest with excitement and fear as he circled over the seven-sided house.

He screamed in ecstasy, "Ajilusgi. I can fly."

He tilted his head back, swept his arms to his side and jettisoned straight up into the sky. His glowing red eyes found the Ani Tsutsa and he decided to visit the seven boys to thank them for sharing their powers with him.

"Wado, Ani Tsutsa. Wado. Wado." He shouted gratefully.

As he rocketed higher and higher, the tiny sparkling stars grew into flaming campfires that illuminated the glowing bodies of the seven boys standing to wave at him. Triumphantly he spread his wings out and tilted his head to one side slowing his ascent and gracefully rolling over to glide downward toward the tiny forests and mountains of Turtle Island, the land of the Cherokee.

Enraptured by his flight, he pulled his arms to his side to feel the total exhilaration of his accelerating dive. Confidently, he spread his arms and pulled up before crashing into the thick forest. He held his position as his flight circled up and over and back down. With a twist of his wrists, he spiraled over and glided above the blackened, shadowy woods where he had grown up. There was the house he grew up in with the flowing stream beside it leading to the palisaded village. There was his aunt's house. He marveled at the beauty of the glowing windows of all the houses in the village. He flew up and past the village, circled, and then swooped down just above the village roof tops.

Involuntarily, he squawked loudly. He recognized the sound he made as that of a raven diving, not the normal squawks. He looked back to see the villagers pouring out of their houses to look up in his wake. Remembering the danger of being spotted by a "seer", he slapped his hands to his side and jettisoned to gain the safety of distance.

His head began swimming and his stomach started feeling nauseous. Reluctantly, he decided to return to the tranquil pond where his hero, his mentor, was waiting proudly for him to return. He extended his arms to slow his flight as the crease in the forest where the familiar stream flowed came into view. As he approached, he pulled his arms up more and more to try to control his speed.

Ker plunk! The plummeting mass impacted into the pond exploding the tranquil waters out of the pond in an enormous circular wave carrying the fragile old wizard up and onto the shore. He sat up quickly in time to see the exposed slimy bottom of the pond with his apprentice sprawled out motionless in a muddy impact crater. As the water rushed back into the void, he was sucked back into the desecrated pond trying to restore itself. Powered by adrenalin, the desperate mentor clamored to find and rescue his student until the thrashing currents tumbled and tossed him in a disorienting maelstrom. He was sure this would be their last day in the center world.

AJILUSGI SMILED THROUGH HER pain and fatigue as she imagined her ebullient adopted child flying through the air as a flaming raven. The boy's ambitious, impetuous enthusiasm was infectious. His happy smile and insatiable curiosity always perked her up and made her feel better if for only a moment. She couldn't wait for him to return to tell her all about his exciting first flight in his impassioned way.

A shaft of soft moonlight streaked across the floor. She looked expectantly, excitedly at the door to see feet poked through hooking the door cover and swiveling to push it to one side. The dark shadow of a drenched, muddy, tall skinny boy carrying a soaked and dripping, disheveled old man was framed in the doorway.

Ajilusgi reflexively tried to rise as she squealed in her raspy voice, "Sge, Galunlati. What has happened?"

She sat panting on the edge of her bed as she watched the lanky boy plop, plop across the floor with the limp old man in his arms.

"He's ok; just needs to dry off and warm up."

Ajilusgi covered her mouth and sucked big gulps of air as she held her throbbing heart with her other hand.

Trembling and totally exhausted, the excited old man managed, "He flew, Mother, he did it."

The embarrassed, but proud boy exclaimed, "I'm going to have to work on my landings. I almost killed us both."

After seven days of intensive training, Ugidahli Unega had reached the end of his rope. The old couple was starting to decline again despite all of his efforts and all of their knowledge of medicines, conjures, and the dark ways of witchcraft. The evenings were the worst. As they sat around the hearth studying the flames, the despondent student looked into the dark, sad eyes of the old man. The reflection of the flames danced in his black, watery eyes. "You've done your best, Ugi, there is nothing more that can be done."

"I don't accept that, Grandfather. There is a solution. We just haven't figured it out yet."

Ajilusgi was seized by a deep, hacking cough that left her exhausted and clutching her ribs. She gasped for several minutes to regain her breath. Ugi leaped to her side and rubbed the hair from her forehead with his palm. "Are you in pain, Grandmother?"

She forced a weak smile and turned her sad, teary eyes to him. "Grandson, there is something that I must tell you before I go to the afterworld."

"You're not going anywhere, Grandmother, I will see to it."

She took his hand and rubbed it tenderly as she struggled to continue, "I'm sure you will, but listen to me, for what I have to tell you means so much to me. I need you to know this."

"Alright, Grandmother, I am listening."

The old woman turned to stare upwards as she framed her words, "Remember that I told you that your grandmother and I were once very close?"

"Yes, Grandmother."

"Well … we were more … we are … were sisters."

Ajilusgi coughed uncontrollably while her shocked young friend gasped and tried to absorb this revelation. His thoughts raced in his head as he rubbed her shoulder sympathetically and tried to calm her down. That was why Ajilusgi had always seemed so familiar. Now he realized that she was almost his grandmother's twin. The expressions; the large, round, kind face; the large frame. It was so obvious that he couldn't believe he had not seen it before.

Her coughing subsided and she continued. "I have not seen … "Aji", as she has come to be called, since we were young girls. When I chose …"

The hesitant woman turned to look at her husband, "… Aji did not approve of Adawehi."

She seemed to be having trouble continuing. Sympathizing, the boy prompted her, "Because he is a witch?"

The thoughtful old woman turned back and looked up again as she pondered his question. "I don't think she knew back then. Maybe she sensed something. Aji was always very perceptive."

Ajilusgi's eyes danced as she lapsed into her memories. Finally, she turned to look at Ugidahli as if she had forgotten he was there. Then she turned back and continued, "I didn't care. I loved Adawehi and so when he brought me the deer as his way of proposing marriage, I accepted his proposal despite her protests."

She turned to the boy to explain, "You see, our grandmother was no longer living, so I could make the decision myself."

"Once Adawehi and I chose the dark path, there was no going back. But I kept track of Aji through the crystals. And I sometimes secretly visited her in raven form."

The reminiscing old woman's eyes danced again at the visions only she could see in front of her. Her confessed nephew glanced up at the empty darkness where her eyes focused and then back to her happy eyes. He waited patiently for her story to continue.

At last, the happiness on her face turned serious and she faced him. "I never met your father, but when I would listen from the trees, I could hear Aji and … your father arguing. Your father was a very strong-willed man. Aji despised your mother and her family. She begged him not to marry her, but he was in love and couldn't see the hornet's nest that he was stepping into."

She shook her head sympathetically, "Poor Aji. First me, then him."

She looked deep into Ugidahli's eyes, "Such a tragic death."

The boy responded, "How did you learn of my father's death?"

Ajilusgi hesitated. Her face showed pain. Adawehi shuffled up beside the bed to comfort her and explain for her, "She saw it in the crystals."

The boy gasped. "You saw my father's death?"

The grieving woman turned away consumed by painful sobs. Adawehi led the astonished boy back to the hearth. "No one should witness such a brutal …"

The old man stopped in mid-sentence. His eyes lit up as if something of great portent had occurred to him.

"Grandfather, what are you thinking?"

Adawehi's answer surprised the young apprentice, "Nunyunuwi."

"Stone Clad? The cannibal?"

The weak old man nodded. "He has been alive forever and is still going strong—strong enough to wear the heavy stone plates and fight like a young warrior."

Ugidahli knew very little about "Stone Clad". His mother had warned him as a child to not go out after dark "or Nunyunuwi will get you and eat you."

He had doubted the existence of such a creature. He had believed it was just some fictional monster made up to scare little children. He HAD believed that until his dead, mutilated father had been returned to the village and he overheard the elder whisper "Nunyunuwi".

"Don't you get it, Ugi?" the old wizard exclaimed excitedly.

Ugi didn't get it. "What, Grandfather, get what?"

"Nunyunuwi knows the secret. He holds the key to immortality."

The sweltering room was exquisitely uncomfortable. Aji hoped it would shorten Awi-e Usdi's stay. She offered him a seat next to the hearth and delighted in watching him hesitate, look back at the door, then reluctantly take his seat.

AJI STOOD IN THE door of her hot hut to cool down. The corpulent, sweating woman rubbed her fat, sticky hands on her thickly woven dress. She stared at the giant oak tree where a curious raven had often visited. The huge bird had hidden in the leafy shadows technically invisible, but she had somehow sensed its presence. Subtle clues had teased her senses and stirred her intuition. She could just somehow feel the eidolon spying on her. It was like a loving pet coming to share the moment with her, giving her companionship and support. It was not there today.

Udo looked up at her curiously for a moment before returning to his laborious task of weaving strands of hemp to produce new twine for his bow.

It had been seven days since Udo had returned with the vexing news that her grandson had not gone home, but had instead sneaked off to live with Ajilusgi. She could not in her heart believe that her sister would poison her grandson's soul with witchcraft. But Udo's description of Aji's use of his necklace concerned her. Priests and medicine men used stones to divine truths, so Ugi may have learned to query the spirits elsewhere. But, it was not normal for the Deer Clan to indulge in these matters.

She had prayed that her sister had done the right thing and sent Ugi home. If only she knew for sure.

"Udo … "

"I'll go check on him, Mother."

Aji nodded, "I'll pack you some cakes."

Ugidahli stuffed the rope into his bulging pack. Adawehi sat on his favorite stump in the shade of the porch rubbing his chin thoughtfully. They had spent the morning devising defensive traps and strategizing. Adawehi had feverishly produced and explained every type of trap he could think of and downloaded every detail and fact about Nunyunuwi he knew. He had jammed potions and medicines into Ugi's bulging pack and reviewed all manner of curse and protective imprecations. Ugidahli had patiently tolerated Adawehi's apprehension, but was now anxious to get on with his quest. Both knew that the venture had little chance of success, but both were determined to give it their best effort and resigned to the fact that it was probably the only chance to save Ajilusgi and Adawehi.

Ugi stood and hefted the pack onto his back. He smiled tentatively at his coach and nodded bravely. Adawehi closed his eyes and reciprocated.

So, that was it, the brave young wizard turned to start his quest.

Aji had busied herself with mindless chores to pass the day. It was midday when her worrying was interrupted by a noisy disturbance in the woods. She jumped up and strode to the doorway. It was too raucous to be a large bear or a pack of wolves or coyotes. It was a group of men approaching. Their tell-tale voices betrayed them.

Aji wiped corn powder off her hands onto her dress and waited for the men to appear. Ahuli appeared from the thick woods beside the house and hid cautiously in the bushes as the four men marched into the clearing in front of the house.

"Osiyo!" the leader greeted as he lifted his palm to indicate peace.

Aji recognized the tall, thin, muscular physique and chiseled face of Awi-e Usdi. His two brothers and a stranger followed. Aji glared at the obstinate man as her son stepped out of the shadows to expose his threat to the intruders.

Awi-e Usdi nodded to Uhuli and then smiled at Aji. Getting no response, he explained, "Ugidahli has run away and we have not seen him for seven days. His mother is very concerned and asked us to search for him."

The tall man fidgeted slightly in the ominous presence of the unflinching woman, "We thought he might have come here."

Ahuli looked at his mother tentatively. Aji turned and lumbered into her house. Awi-e Usdi glanced at his companions a bit perplexed, shrugged and then followed the woman inside. The brothers and the stranger traded glares with Uhuli. Ugowe glided in from behind the flustered men, "Come sit," he offered matter-of-factly, breaking the tension.

Ugidahli had almost reached the forbidden forest where Adawehi and Ajilusgi calculated he would find the dreaded cannibal giant Nunyunuwi. That is when the gravity of his endeavor hit him. If detected by the giant, what chance would a novice witch have against the most formidable witch in all of the world? Nunyunuwi had hundreds of years of experience over him not to mention that he was invincible physically.

A wide, shallow river lay before him and beyond that the forbidden forest where many unfortunate hunters, including his father, had met a terrible fate at the hands of the cannibal. He decided that he would build his camp opposite the river from the forbidden forest and cross early the next morning. There was just enough daylight left to set some defensive traps around the perimeter of his camp.

The novice witch waded into the river and, using a new trick Ajilusgi had taught him, he held the crystal just below the flowing waters of the river. He whispered the conjure that called upon the spirits of light to illuminate "the person of interest." The water flowing over the facets of the crystal created many shadowy images. With practice, he had learned to discern the patterns and recognize the image he was requesting. Ugidahli turned the crystal to and fro studying the flickering images. Suddenly, there he was. The monster cannibal was leaning against his cave wall sleeping peacefully. The viewer breathed a sigh of relief before returning back to prepare his camp. Tomorrow would be a big day, but tonight promised to be the most frightening night of his life.

The sweltering room was exquisitely uncomfortable. Aji hoped it would shorten Awi-e Usdi's stay. She offered him a seat next to the hearth and delighted in watching him hesitate, look back at the door, then reluctantly take his seat. Wiping his brow, he glanced about the hearth. Aji followed his eyes wondering what he might be searching for, then remembered that the elite expected to smoke during even a casual council.

"We have no tobacco," she explained.

"Oh, … well … alright, then." Awi-e Usdi shifted uncomfortably, wiped his brow again, and began, "Ugi and his mother had a … disagreement. Ganvnvi discovered that he had somehow acquired a rather elaborate necklace and when he was unable to explain where he acquired it, she demanded he return it."

The uncomfortable guest wiped his sweat-soaked face again. Aji let a droplet of sweat drip from the tip of her nose refusing to lend any attention to her own discomfort. She had noticed the beautiful necklace her grandson was wearing. She had marveled at its uniqueness but had not commented on it. Now she wished that she had questioned him about it. Her guest continued, "When he had not returned the following day, Ganvnvi came to me with her concern. I tried to assure her that he had gone home and would be fine, but when she persisted, I went to their old home and found the boy lodging there."

Aji smiled at the irony.

"We expected that he would soon return to the village, but when the days passed and he didn't return, I once again checked the old house only to find that it was vacant and there was no sign that Ugi was staying there any longer."

Awi-e Usdi turned his cloth searching for a dry spot. Unable to find one, he attempted to wipe his face with the soaked rag. Afterwards, he shrugged, "We hoped he might be here."

Aji shifted. She couldn't help feeling sorry for the pitiful man. Besides, she needed some time to construct her reply, "Perhaps it would be more comfortable outside."

Gratefully, the miserable guest jumped up and fled to the cool of outdoors. Aji rolled over and pushed herself up, took a deep breath and fluttered the neck of her dress to fan her sweaty body. As she waddled toward the door, she stopped to grab a cloth, lifted her dress and swathed her stomach and around her breasts. She knew she could not divulge the whereabouts of Ugi. Technically, she didn't know for sure herself. She took a deep breath and stepped outside not knowing what she would say. She needed to come up with something that would not only protect Ugi, but would also satisfy his mother and uncle temporarily until she could get the matter resolved.

She found Awi-e Usdi standing in the middle of the clearing swiping his neck with the soggy cloth. His two brothers and the stranger were sitting cross-legged in the shade of the porch. Her sons were sitting quietly on stumps next to them. They were not engaged in conversation, just patiently biding their time while the principals hashed things out.

Aji fluttered the neck of her dress as she strolled across the clearing to stand next to Awi-e Usdi. The draft created by her waving dress cooled her sweating body slightly. She considered suggesting they continue their conversation in the river, then smiled at the idiocy of the idea.

With her back to the others, she confided, "Ugi has been here."

The startled uncle glanced about, "Where is he?"

She continued, "He is not here now. Hopefully, he and Udo will return in a day or so."

The uncle stirred the dirt with his foot and the muscles in his temples rippled with suppressed anger. "Why have you been keeping him from his mother?"

This angered Aji, but she managed to control herself. "I sent him home days ago, but he went to the old home instead … as you know. He refuses to go back, but I think I can change his mind if you will give me some time."

Awi-e Usdi shifted around, clearly weighing his options, he maintained his silence. He glared at the old rickety hut. He glared at the path where they had entered the compound. He glared at Aji's strong, barrel-chested sons. He glared at his wimpy brothers. He glared at the towering woman steadfast in her resolve. He glared at the heavens that offered no assistance. At last, he paused, took a deep breath and nodded his acceptance. He then turned to his companions and nodded for them to join him. Without any further word, they marched back into the woods.

CHAPTER

24

The last thing he remembered was coaxing himself to stay awake by reviewing the description Adawehi had given of the stone clad giant. Adawehi told Ugi that Nunyunuwi had once invaded his village when he was very young. News that he was coming raced through the village instilling fear in everyone. The women quickly gathered up their children while the men gathered up their weapons. Although only twelve summers old, Adawehi broke away from his mother to join the men to fight the monster. He said he would never forget seeing the monster for the first time. Stone Clad was a giant. Twice as tall as any man he had ever seen. He must have been stronger than ten men, too, because his body was covered with huge stone plates. No arrows could penetrate the plates. And any warrior that tried to battle the giant with his hatchet was knocked away like a fly. The determined warrior-monster swiftly battled through the futile village warriors to chase down the fleeing women.

A young virgin was snatched up by Stone-Clad who then fled into the forest and disappeared. The village mourned their lost daughter. The elders speculated that the girl would have been raped, murdered, and then eaten by the monster.

The sound "snap"and "swish" woke Ugidahli, he wondered how long he had been sleeping. It was the tree snare. He had caught something. A childish, tenor voice began cursing and then yelled for help. *Is that wimpy voice how the giant cannibal witch sounds?*

"Wake up, Ugi, help me." the wimpy voice persisted.

Ugi checked his war club lying beside him and clutched the knife in its scabbard on his waist belt. Carefully he pushed away the branches and leaves he had pulled on top of him for camouflage.

"IIIIEEEEEEE. Wake up you lazy scamp. Get me down from here. Ugi, help!"

The night air was damp and the moon was still high in the night sky. He could hear the taut rope squeaking as it swung back and forth with its prey. It was clearly not Nunyunuwi caught in the snare. Ugi pushed through the thick underbrush, readied his war club and peeked through to see a tiny little man with one ankle snared in the rope hanging upside down, kicking and flailing with his long hair swishing back and forth as he swung out and back. "Nvwoti? What are you doing here?"

He had snared his childhood Yunwi Tsunsdi friend. Ugi dropped his war club and raced to his friend's aide. He leaped up and grabbed a handful of the tiny man's long, flowing, silver hair pulling him down but not enough to stop his swinging leaving them both dangling and swinging, kicking and flailing.

"Ouch. That's my hair you brain of a worm sucking bird."

Ugi ignored the insult and pulled down hard on his friend's hair, so that he could grab the snared man's necklace to pull himself up further. This had the added benefit of choking off his rude expletives. Releasing his hair, he grabbed the strangling man's belt with his other hand but from there the only option for the rescuer was to climb up the little man's body like shimmying up a tree trunk. Finally, he had climbed high enough to reach the rope. As the two struggling friends bounced up and down, and back and forth, Ugi managed to cut the rope dropping them abruptly onto the dwarf's head.

The stunned little man lay flat on his back with his arms outstretched and mouth open. Ugi rolled off the tiny man's body, spun around and grabbed his narrow shoulders. He was certain the little man was dead until his eyes popped open, eyebrows furrowed, steely eyes glared at his rescuer and mouth snarled before screaming a renewed tirade of profanities.

The relieved boy rolled over onto his back, clutching his stomach, consumed with laughter. His mirth was ended abruptly by the stinging pop to his nose by the offended Yunwi Tsunsdi's fist.

"Ow."

The two bruised and bedraggled friends sat up and took stock of their condition. The tall boy wiped a trickle of blood from his upper lip while the little man used both hands to pop the crick out of his neck.

"What are you doing here, Nvwoti Atlisdodi?"

The little man stretched his arms above his head to pop his shoulders back into place, "Trying to rescue your stupid butt."

Ugidahli chuckled, "Nice job."

The angry little man showed the ingrate his fist. "That's the appreciation I get for risking my life for an imbecile, ignoramus, numskull."

The ignoramus numskull hissed his contempt for the unwelcomed intruder. "YOU were going to save ME from a GIANT?"

The wiry little man tackled the disrespectful boy knocking him on his back while he climbed up on his chest and pressed his miniature fist on the surprised boy's tender nose.

"Okay, okay, I apologize," the boy feigned.

Suddenly, there was a loud "whop" and the compact body of the Yunwi Tsunsdi went tumbling into the bushes beside the two cohorts. A huge hand grasped the throat of the feigning boy and jerked him up toward the sky. Ugidahli Unega found himself looking down into the fierce, glowing, red eyes of a huge, snarling face. The scrappy compact body came flying out of the bushes punching, biting and kicking the shin of the giant attacker. The giant attacker kicked the tiny warrior attacking his shin, sending him head over heels back into the bushes. With a deep, resounding roar, the giant bolted off toward the river with Ugidahli dangling from his hand. The dwarf scrambled out of the bushes again and raised his fist shouting, "Come back you coward. Fight like a man," as he scampered off after them.

Ugidahli Unega's consciousness had been squeezed away by the enormous, powerful hand of his kidnapper somewhere in the struggle. As his consciousness returned he found himself bound and lying on his side beside the massive hearth and glowing embers of Nunyunuwi's cavernous lair.

The dank smell of a poorly ventilated, stale cave; the stench of bat guano; the strong odor of burnt wood combined to attack his senses. It was cool and damp in the cave as Ugi surveyed his situation. The giant cannibal did not appear to be around. The room he was in was large and domed with branching tunnels at either end. His throat was raw and felt restricted. When he swallowed, it was painful and difficult. The sides of his neck ached. His face was stinging and felt tight especially around the right cheek bone. His arms ached and he felt excruciating pain in his abdomen. The dust of the cave floor tickled his throbbing throat and prompting him to cough. It sent daggers of pain into his lower chest cavity and burning in his throat. He drew up into a tight fetal position.

"Psst."

The hiss came from above him. Pulling his head back, he strained to pin-point its location. The dwarf was hiding behind a rock near the cave wall. "You okay?"

He was not okay. He pulled his head down and tried to nurture his painful body. A few moments later, he felt a tingling in his bound wrists and realized that his gallant friend was attempting to untie him. He surveyed the lair wondering which of the numerous tunnels led to the entrance. He felt the ropes tugging and twisting as his courageous little friend desperately sawed them with his knife.

"Where is he?" he whispered.

"Must have smelled another victim. He pointed his cane, smelled the tip of it and rushed out."

Snap. His hands were free and the Yunwi Tsunsdi handed him the knife so he could cut the bindings on his ankles while his little rescuer trotted to one of the tunnel exits to watch for Nunyunuwi.

Snap. He was free. The sharp pain in his stomach halted his first attempt to stand. The dwarf galloped by motioning urgently for him to follow. He pushed through the pain to follow his little friend as he scampered into a darkening tunnel. As they raced around a bend in the tunnel, his friend stopped abruptly. They faced a dead end. Nvwoti glanced about confused.

"You're lost." the boy hissed angrily.

The tiny man galloped off in a new direction but slowed as he realized this branch was opening up instead of narrowing into the entrance opening. Before them was a ledge with the deep blackness of a large pit beyond. Ugidahli reversed and started running back toward the flickering light of the fire. Tiny boney fingers grabbed his belt and pulled him to one side. A ferocious roar confirmed that the cannibal had returned and had discovered that his prisoner had escaped. Ugidahli watched his little friend scurry back toward the dark pit and followed. As they stood before the edge, they faced jumping into the darkness or returning to face the monster. They jumped.

The desperate, fleeing companions landed on a slimy, sloping embankment almost immediately. They tumbled and rolled down the slope until it leveled out leaving them sprawling on the slate floor. They paused for a moment to collect themselves, and then the glow from a torch approached the ledge above. The improving light illumi-nated a tunnel nearby and they scurried into it. The tunnel was long but a tiny shaft of light shown from its end.

They pressed their bodies up against the slippery wall of the tunnel, held their breaths and listened and watched. The dim light falling across the entrance to their tunnel from above was fading as did the weak light in the pit. They carefully peered up at the ledge from the entrance of the tunnel. The light was dimming because the monster was leaving. They continued to press back against the wall until the only light left came from the other end of the tunnel. Quietly they slipped to the end of the tunnel. The shaft of light was shining between two large stones narrowly perched on top of a large pile of stones that had fallen from the ceiling, blocking the exit.

Quietly and carefully, they began restacking the stones behind them until they had removed enough stones to squeeze through. The bright morning light was warm and inviting but the escapees feared that Nunyunuwi could be lurking outside waiting for them. The Yunwi Tsunsdi winked at his hesitant companion, and magically faded away. Ugidahli smiled as his invisible friend scrambled through the narrow opening. He waited intensely for the "all clear" signal.

As Ugidahli strained his eyes to detect signs of his invisible little friend, he felt a hot breeze across his neck. Without thinking, he rubbed his neck only to feel the breeze on the back of his hand. It stopped for a moment and then came again. Puzzled, he turned and found himself looking into the glowing red eyes of the monster. Startled, he responded instinctively, leaping away to scratch and claw his way out the narrow opening while kicking and wriggling to stay free of the grasping hands of the beast still trapped behind the stack of stones they had removed from the exit. Tumbling down the pile of stones, Ugi ignored the stabbing pain in his ribs and the bruises and scrapes from the jagged stones. He kicked away from the reaching fingers of his assailant, emerged from the entrance and scrambled to his feet to race into the forest leaving the giant still pinned behind the narrow opening. The gut-wrenching roar from the frustrated cannibal monster filled the valleys and echoed off the surrounding mountains. Ugidahli Unega raced on blindly.

CHAPTER

25

IT WAS AROUND MID-MORNING when a breathless Udo burst into the clearing and collapsed under the porch beside his anxious mother. Between gulps for air, he struggled to deliver his message, "He ... has ... been ... captured!"

Aji gasped from shock. Her other three sons magically appeared and gathered around their exhausted brother.

"Captured?" Aji prompted.

"By the ... monster ... Nunyunuwi!"

His brothers glancing at each other, shocked and surprised, sharing their concern. The oldest pressed him, "Where?"

Udo pointed generally northwest and desperately added, "We ... must save him ..."

Before he could say more, his brothers bolted into the house to grab their weapons. Aji scrambled inside to snatch cornbread cakes for their packs. Within just a few heart beats, the four brothers were racing back into the woods.

Ugidahli dove behind a stack of boulders and rolled into the pinon trees rooted in the side of the huge rocks. He scrambled to his knees and peeked out at the mound covering Nunyunuwi's cave. The monster came racing around the base of the mound, stopped, glanced all about, raised his fist and roared. Ugidahli ducked and cringed as if the blast from the monster's roar might blow him out of his hiding place.

He looked back to see the monster point his cane in his direction, smell the tip, smile and race toward him. Ugi looked all around him trying to decide what to do as the giant cannibal bounded closer and closer. He forced his aching body to leap over the boulders and tumbled down the other side. He managed to scramble to his feet and race into the thick woods in front of him. He could hear the roar of Nunyunuwi closing in behind him as he climbed the steep slope of a cliff hidden in the woods.

As he approached the summit, he realized that the giant had grown quiet. He carefully pushed back a bush to view the monster. Nunyunuwi had stopped at the bottom of the cliff and was glancing all around attracted by the raspy calls of hawks or ravens coming from the peaks surrounding him. After each caw, the cannibal pointed his cane in its direction and then smelled the tip. As soon as he started after that distraction, a loud, taunting caw could be heard on an opposite peak provoking the giant to check it with his cane.

And so it went, back and forth, to and fro until the exasperated giant finally decided to concentrate on one and ignore all others. Soon the giant had crossed the river that bordered the forbidden forest and disappeared into the woods.

Ugidahli sat back and breathed a sigh of relief. At least for now, the monster was in pursuit of someone or something else. He chuckled to himself as he postulated that his friend Nvwoti Atlisdodi had probably come to his rescue once again. Late into the evening he could hear the roars of the frustrated giant chasing his eidolons.

Defeated and resigned, Ugidahli Unega sat alone on a boulder surrounded by a cover of trees atop a hill overlooking his camp site. Through the branches of the trees, he watched Nunyunuwi dance and shout around the fire he had set to burn all of the potions, food, utensils, weapons and blankets he found around the camp. The bitter onlooker cursed the seemingly invincible adversary. All of the preparation he and Adawehi had made for his quest was now going up in smoke. Grand potions to make the giant weak, or vulnerable, or sick, or sleepy, destroyed; antidotes and concoctions to make Ugidahli stronger, or more perceptive, or swifter, or smarter, all gone.

"That stuff wouldn't have worked against Nunyunuwi anyway."

The voice seemed to be emanating from the boulder itself. Slowly, the image of Nvwoti materialized sitting solemnly beside his despondent companion. He held up Ugidahli's prized necklace, "I saved your necklace."

"Wado." The boy lifted the necklace over his head gratefully.

The two sat in silence watching the jubilant giant celebrate. "I don't know why he's celebrating. We both got away."

The Yunwi Tsunsdi giggled. The Little People were naturally a happy, playful people drumming and dancing day and night. They loved to play tricks on wandering travelers or hunters. When molested by unwelcome visitors, they were known to put a curse on them leaving them disoriented and lost.

"Can't you put one of your curses on him to make him confused?"

Again the little man giggled and then explained, "His medicine is too strong."

"He must have some weakness."

The tiny man jumped up and began dancing around his irritated friend singing,

> Hi ganu, hi ganu, hi ganu yahi.
> The man of stone, can hold his own,
> against all mortal men.
> Hi ganu, hi ganu. Hi ganu yahi.
> He's cursed to heed, the chaste who bleed,
> on that you can depend. …

Ugidahli tried to snatch the taunting dancer but he was too quick and nimble. So, he let the menacing little trickster continue his taunts until he ran down. He knew that Nvwoti Atlisdodi was quickly bored.

When the fun of the taunt finally waned, the childish heckler stood beside his friend and put his arm around him as if to console him. Putting on his "serious" face, he began a story, "Many, many years ago, before anyone alive today remembers, Nunyunuwi made the mistake of capturing what he supposed to be a pretty young virgin. After ravaging her and as he was strangling her, the witch dropped her façade. The stunned rapist staggered away and purged his stomach. The triumphant witch cackled and taunted the repulsed assailant and placed a curse on him."

The happy story teller resumed his heckling dance and song to the dismay of his audience, "Hi ganu, Hi ganu …"

"So, what's the curse?" Ugidahli interrupted.

The dancer stopped, put his hands on his hips proudly and declared, "From that day forward, he would lose all of his strength and powers in the presence of a menstruating virgin."

Ugidahli was furious, "You waited until now to tell me that?"

The Yunwi Tsunsdi was offended, "That's what I came to tell you last night before you tried to kill me with your snares. I didn't exactly have a chance to tell you, did I?"

Ugidahli was silent. The devious little man studied his young friend, "You don't even know what a menstruating virgin is, do you?"

He fell down on the stone laughing at his naïve friend.

"Of course I know. You can't study the medicines without hearing all about the unclean condition of women. I know how to treat all of the manifestations—the cramps, the headaches, the heavy bleeding, the …"

"OK, ok, so you know." the repulsed little taunter interrupted.

"What I don't know is where to find one." the learned witch-in-training admitted.

His taunter felt reprieved. He fell back into his irritating chortling again. Then he lay back with hands behind his head smiling proudly. Slowly, he began to fade away, infuriating Ugidahli. "You're not going to tell me?"

Before his eyes, Nvwoti faded away leaving Ugidahli alone with his mixed feelings. He was excited about the knowledge that Nunyunuwi had a weakness. At least there was a chance he could be defeated. But he was at a loss how to use this new information. *Where do I find one?*

The naïve boy heard cackling behind him. He turned to find his friend holding his stomach and rolling on the ground again. He really wanted to punt the pint-sized smart-aleck off the boulder, but plopped down dejectedly on the rock instead. He could really hate the little man if he didn't love him so much—or at least need him so much.

The little wizard lay out on his back, placed his hands behind his head, crossed his legs, smiled triumphantly, "Don't worry, my friend, the virgin you seek you will find in the asi. It's where they go in their time."

His will and connection with the world were severed by her touch and her existence. He had lost his identity and purpose and followed her blindly into the clearing that lay before the familiar pond and waterfall.

The clouds to the west were dark blue with fiery, bright orange edges. Sister Sun was concealed behind the clouds as she opened the door to her house at the end of the world. Excited and renewed, Ugidahli Unega leaped off the back side of the boulder so he would not be seen by the reveling cannibal. With Ajilusgi's health failing, it was a race against time to save her so he intended to use the tools given him by Adawehi to shape shift into the raven and fly back to the village to search for that special virgin that Nvwoti advised would be waiting in an Asi.

As darkness replaced the day, Ugidahli ripped the Aholiyehvsgi root out of the ground. He looked apprehensively at the sky hoping the clouds would not block the cluster of seven spirit campfires belonging to the seven boys.

She had not noticed the beauty of the colorful sunset nor appreciated the cool breeze that had lifted the muggy heat as darkness settled in. Oblivious to the screaming frogs and fiddling cicadas, Aji's thoughts were in another place where her sons and grandson faced evil and certain death. She imagined every possible horrible fate and dreamed up every possible successful outcome; only time would confirm which of her many scenarios had played out. She feared that the only way she would ever find out, was to make the journey herself. Fretting over how long she should wait before starting that journey, she looked up at the darkening sky and glimpsed a sparkling star streak across the horizon. Perhaps the cover of darkness would be better for investigating the fate of her loved ones? She shook her head. Fearing she was too old to navigate the woods and hills in the darkness, she decided to wait for first light.

A distant rustling in the forest caught her attention. She clasped her hands between her breasts and stood to listen better. Her heart pounded as she dared hope it was the noisy return of her sons … and maybe her grandson. As the racket grew louder, she became more and more certain it was the careless clamoring of humans running through the woods. Suddenly, her four sons broke through the edge of the clearing and gathered round her breathing heavily. The youngest offered his positive message first, "Ugi escaped!"

Aji clapped happily and then realized that Ugi was absent. There was more. She clasped her hands and turned to her oldest son. He could be depended upon for the no-nonsense version.

Ugowe took a slow, deep breath. "Perhaps we should sit at the hearth. We are very tired and there is a lot to tell."

Aji would have none of it, "Where is Ugi?"

Ugowe looked into her desperate eyes with sad foreboding. "Ugi has become the raven. He shape-shifted before our eyes and flew into the sky."

Aji raised her fists to the sky and screamed in agony, "Noooo!"

Beside each house in the village there was a mound known as an Asi. Underneath the plaster mound that constituted the roof was a deep pit with a hearth in the center. The dugout provided a warm and cozy wintering house. But, it was also used year-round for cleansing ceremonies. The men used it to sweat the toxins from their skins. The women retired to the Asi during their time of the month. During those times, the women were considered unclean and were forbidden to touch food or any objects to prevent them from transferring the uncleanliness.

The raven-disguised witch scoured the village for an Asi with a fire burning. This time of year and this time of night, the Asi would only be occupied by a woman. There were five little mounds with smoke rising from their glowing smoke holes. Now the trick would be to find one occupied by a virgin.

A dark shadow crawled out of one of the Asi's and headed for village entrance. Ugidahli whispered the conjure of termination and shape-shifted back into his human form. As the unsuspecting shadow passed under the tree, Ugidahli sneaked down to the ground to follow her.

Ugidahli waited patiently outside of her private place for her to finish. When she emerged from the bushes, he was startled to see that the shadow belonged to the beautiful Tlvdatsi Sakonige; the lithesome beauty from the strawberry patch; the chimera from the pond; the girl of his fantasies. His resolve dissolved. He shrank back into the darkness as she passed. How could he use Sakonige for bait against Nunyunuwi? He couldn't. He would have to return to the tree and watch for another victim.

"Osiyo, Ugidahli Unega."

Ugidahli Unega lurched and audibly gasped as he jumped to his feet, "Sako … Sakonige."

The confident maiden smiled at the shaken stalker.

"I haven't seen you in a while. I heard you ran away."

The runaway wanted to flee again. The unshaken girl stared into his eyes paralyzing him. After an uncomfortably long stare, she calmly strolled up to the paralytic, took him by the hand and led him into the darkness of the forest.

"Why did you come back?" She asked teasingly.

By the way she asked the question, it led him to believe she thought she knew the answer. What should he tell her? *I've come to kidnap you and use you to trick a giant cannibal into telling me his secret to immortality.* Clearly, he couldn't tell her his true reason. He did not answer. She did not push him further as they strolled deeper into the woods in silence.

Being next to her, holding her hand, made him feel queasy and numb. They seemed to be surrounded by a dreamy sphere of surreality while outside the sphere lay empty nothingness. Consciousness lay only within the sphere. His will and connection with the world were severed by her touch and her existence. He had lost his identity and purpose and followed her blindly into the clearing that lay before the familiar pond and waterfall.

As they sat on the flat stone in the darkness before the rippling pond, the sphere drained away and he began to sense the "now" in a way he never had before. His senses came roaring back to him with an intensity he had not experienced before. But, unfortunately, his brain was still malfunctioning.

"I have returned for you."

She smiled and commented, "That's nice."

He could see that she did not understand, "I have come back to take you with me."

She gasped and then giggled patronizingly, "Aren't you sweet?"

Ugidahli was now getting irritated. He grabbed her arm, "I'm serious."

Her face grimaced as she jerked her arm away. She glared at him in a way that he could see that she was both surprised and appalled by his action. She bolted from the rock and tried to flee. He grabbed her arm again and jerked her back. As she spun around she slapped his faced and then wrenched his hand from her arm. She scowled at him as if daring him to touch her again.

"You must come with me, Sakonige, it's critical."

She sneared at him and tilted her head to one side, "What's so … critical?"

He was getting desperate, "I can't tell you."

"Pfew." She hissed in contempt, turned and stomped away.

Infuriated, he grabbed her shoulders and she twisted to free herself and began kicking and struggling. He was amazed by her wiry strength and agility. She squirmed loose and began screaming, "Leave me alone. You're crazy. IIIIIIEEEE."

"Shut up." he whispered worried that her screams could be heard in the village. He cupped his hand and reached for her mouth to muffle her, but caught her chin with his palm. Her eyes rolled up and she crumpled to the ground striking her head on the flat stone.

"Sakonige!" he pleaded as he knelt beside her. He reached behind her head to raise her up. Her hair was soaked. He pulled his wet, sticky hand back out. In the moonlight, he could see his hand covered by a dark liquid. He knew it was blood.

"No! Sakonige. Speak to me." He shook her limp body but she did not wake up. He looked all about him searching for what to do. He collapsed on the flat stone and buried his shameful face in his hands.

CHAPTER

27

His shoulder and back burned with pain as he managed the last few steps to the top of the hill. The chilling night air burned in his sore, aching neck. Exhausted, he dumped the listless body to the ground and fell down beside her. Breathing heavily he looked back toward the village. It was just at the bottom of the hill. With dozens of hills to go, he determined that he could not continue trying to carry his unconscious cargo. Visions of panthers flashed in his head. Images of them leaping onto him as he carried the girl on his shoulders made him shiver. It was critical that she carry herself the rest of the journey. There was no other way. He would have to cure her.

It was difficult finding the plants he needed in the dim moonlight. He hoped that he was lucky. Quickly, he made a mud and leaves compound for her head and wrapped it with strips ripped from her dress. He would need a stream to wash the wound and prepare the potions. Re-invigorated, he raised the unconscious girl into a sitting position, took her wrists, turned and pulled her up onto his back, pulling her arms around him in a false embrace.

At least the journey to the stream would be downhill. With her toes dragging the ground behind him, he headed down the hill.

Battling against time; worried that the next heart beat might be Ajilusgi's last; worried that soon the village would realize that Sakonige was missing; worried that the moon would soon drop so low as to leave him in complete darkness—Ugidahli was driven to work fast and exploit all the skills and knowledge of the medicine he had acquired.

With the last conjure imprecated and the last potion applied, the exuberant wonder boy, the witch wannabe, dropped to his knees and rolled over onto his back. All he could do at that point was to wait for the magic to happen. As he relaxed and tried to recapture his breath, his restless mind relived every word of every conjure and every portion in every potion he had made that night. It was his first real application of medicine on his own.

He went over it again and again.

The pesky fly landed on the greasy proboscis and rubbed its hind legs enthusiastically. The sleeping human swatted his tickled nose and then jumped up startled and breathing heavily. It was still dark but a light dome was building in the east. He had fallen asleep. Now full awake, he glanced at the recuperating body lying next to him. She was sleeping so peacefully and naturally that he could not resist leaning over and kissing her forehead. As he pulled away, she opened her eyes, smiled warmly and looked lovingly up at him. He was so relieved that the anomaly didn't register at first. When it did register, he was scared. Something was wrong, terribly wrong. This girl who should be fleeing from him was, instead, looking at him as if he were the man of her dreams.

"How do you feel?"

Sakonige dreamily fluttered her eyes at him, "I'm fine."

Ugidahli frowned as he tenderly removed the mud pack from her head. He turned her head gently with his thumb and examined the back of her head like a chimp picking flees. He could find no sign of her injury. As he removed his busy fingers from her hair, his patient lazily turned back to smile at him appreciatively.

His internal alarm clock went off. Time was wasting.

"We have to get moving." He whispered as his eyes searched the hillside for villagers. There was no detectible movement along the trail.

He helped the languorous girl stand. That's when he noticed that the plant he had thought was Five Finger Sang to treat her for her head injury was actually Burseed. Which meant instead of curing head pain, he had given her a … love potion.

He looked at the miss-medicated girl and realized that this was the best mistake of his life. Why hadn't he thought of it? What better way to get this independent girl to follow him into the lair of a monster?

Ugidahli was about to lose his patience. Sakonige just had no sense of urgency. She strolled along as if they had all day and nowhere to go while Ajilusgi might be just one breath away from death. She was totally relaxed and fearless while they were about to face the most evil, invincible, cannibal witch to ever live, one who enjoyed ravaging virgins and eating hunters.

"Sakonige. Come on, keep up."

The lovely girl smiled warmly and casually strolled forward a few steps, noticed a pretty flower and stopped to scoop it up with both hands and inhale its fragrance.

"Ooo. You have to smell this one, Ugi; it's so sweet. Look. Isn't it beautiful?"

Frustrated, he stomped over to his distracted companion, gave a quick, obliging whiff of the flower, grabbed her hand and dragged her behind him. Expecting her to resist, the love-struck girl stumbled happily along with her prescribed love interest. She was in a world of blissful infatuation and all the world had taken on a new level of beauty. "Ugi. Can you smell it?"

The man on a mission looked back frustrated, "Smell what?"

"The smells of the forest are crisper and sweeter. The foliage is greener and lusher. Look at the vivid reflections in the dew drops dripping from the vibrant leaves."

Ugidahli frowned and continued dragging his mystified captive forward.

"Oh! Look at the sparkling and intricately woven spider web stretched across the dark gap of the path. How proud the spider must be to have discovered such a busy location to entrap his prey. And how ambitious the little critter must be to place his snare where large animals, thousands of times his size, frequent. But, oh, how wonderful if he could snare a deer—he would be set for life."

Ugidahli plowed on through the forest rushing to his appointment with destiny. Furiously, he wiped the sticky cobweb remnants from his face. Sakonige giggled, "Oh, poor little spider. He had such high hopes."

The unappreciative escaped prey frowned at his silly girlfriend, "What are you babbling about?"

"You just don't realize how lucky you are."

The lucky but irritated boyfriend shook his head and jerked the distracted girlfriend back into their quest. He set his mind to recall some potion that would light a fire under his impassive accomplice.

The evil witch continued, "It is easy to kill a raven and eat his tasty heart, liver, and bones, but can you kill a man and do the same?"

Sᴀᴋᴏɴɪɢᴇ ᴡᴇᴀʀɪʟʏ ᴘʟᴏᴘᴘᴇᴅ ᴅᴏᴡɴ obediently on the mossy stone next to the rushing stream as Ugidahli pulled the crystal from its netted pouch in his necklace. Squatting in the stream, he held the sparkling quartz just beneath a bulging flow while he studied the flickering images and muttered the conjure to reveal "the one of interest." As he carefully adjusted the angle of the crystal the unsteady image of Nunyunuwi materialized. The imposing monster stood pointing his stone cane and glaring into Ugidahli's eyes. The image gave him a start. He quickly gazed about him. *Is Nunyunuwi actually looking at me?*

Satisfied that the monster was nowhere near, he resumed viewing the crystal. The Giant pulled back his cane and smelled its tip and then began laughing haughtily as if he had just played a joke on someone. Behind the massive man, Ugidahli could see his cave entrance. The arrogant monster turned and lumbered into his lair.

Ugidahli quickly called upon the spirits for safety and then grabbed Sakonige's hand. "Come on, it's time to face the monster."

Sakonige limply fell in behind her determined champion, "Monster?"

There it was, the unpretentious cave entrance of Nunyunuwi.

"Oh, look, Ugi, a cave. Can we explore it?"

Stunned by her naïve request, Ugi smiled deviously, "Good idea."

As they entered the lair of the monster, Ugi whispered, "Let me go in first and then you follow."

Sakonige smiled playfully with bright, eager eyes and patted her fingers together as she stomped her happy feet. Ugidahli took a deep breath, stood tall and strolled gallantly into the cloister of death. He found Nunyunuwi sitting casually by his hearth leaning against the curved wall of the vaulted chamber smiling confidently at the neophyte. "I've been expecting you."

The imposing giant laughed pompously. Ugidahli shivered involuntarily, his confidence slipping away.

But the arrogant smile of the giant faded and his bearing changed as the wonderstruck beauty strolled up timidly to cradle her companion's arm and stare curiously at the giant.

"What is this?" the terrified giant bellowed.

Ugidahli smiled confidently. "Perhaps a curse?"

Gasping for breath and clutching his chest, the cursed Giant whispered, "Get her away from me."

Ugidahli inched forward dragging his reluctant accomplice along, desperately attached to his arm. The novice witch spoke in a presumed wizardly voice, "I do not seek to harm you. I come seeking that which only you possess. We will leave forthwith, but first you must share with me that which I seek to resuscitate my friends from the clutches of death."

The wavering giant acknowledged, "Adawehi and Ajilusgi."

Slightly unnerved by the giant's cognizance, he nodded and explained, "I seek for them the secret of immortality that only you possess."

Nunyunuwi eyed the resolute young man skeptically. A trickle of blood ran down his chin from the corner of his mouth. "Nothing else motivates you?"

Ugidahli stood firm and stared confidently into the giant's eyes. The enfeebled immortal squinted challengingly at the diffident boy, unconvinced. "You don't harbor any motives for revenge?"

Ugidahli drew confidence from the splatters of blood the giant spat with each word. Clearly the curse was working. He understood that Nunyunuwi suspected he might also want to avenge his father's death. "Today my only concern is for my dying friends. It is too late to rescue my father."

The giant was unwavering. Ugidahli, with Sakonige in tow, advanced toward the obstinate witch. The witch's face contorted and he hunched over in pain spewing blood. Ugidahli pulled his knife and clinched his teeth in anger, "Tell me what I request. You have no choice. You have my word that I do not seek revenge. But do not doubt that if you resist, I will surely kill you."

He felt Sakonige tug on his arm, "Ugi, I think I want to go home now."

"Shhh!" Ugi hissed with such absolute authority that he made Sakonige fear him more than the bleeding giant. The debilitated giant nodded his agreement to divulge the secret and waved them back with a limp hand. Ugidahli peeled Sakonige's hands from his arm, "Go stand by the entrance."

The terrified girl resisted and attempted to re-grasp his arm, "It's ok, Sakonige, he cannot harm you."

The stunned, doubtful girl backed away from her protector slowly keeping her eyes pinned on the hunched over giant. The further she moved away the more the cannibal's apparent pain subsided. Ugidahli motioned for her to stop as he moved in to face the giant, "Now, Nunyunuwi, explain the secret."

The suffering man coughed blood as he tried to catch his breath to speak. Ugidahli pressed his knife to the balking man's throat.

"Adawehi actually came very close to discovering the secret himself," the sadistic witch chuckled at the thought. Ugidahli pressed the knife deeper.

Nunyunuwi sucked in a precious breath of air, "He would never have gotten it, though, he doesn't have the stomach to do what is required."

Ugidahli's patience was waning, "What is required?" he yelled.

The witch held up his hand defensively, then glared at the impatient boy, "Can YOU kill a man for his souls?"

Ugidahli pulled back slightly, but stood his ground.

The evil witch continued, "It is easy to kill a raven and eat his tasty heart, liver, and bones, but can you kill a man and do the same?"

Ugidahli sneered at the cruel man as his eyes teared and his hands began to tremble, "I could kill you."

The contemptuous giant laughed perversely then gagged as Ugidahli pressed the knife firmer against his throat pricking the skin causing droplets of blood to ooze out. The perverse man reached for his throat and waved his assailant back off as he pointed to his throat and then his mouth to communicate that he couldn't speak. Ugidahli obliged.

As the exhausted man rubbed his punctured throat, and spit a wad of blood from his mouth, he continued, "There are four askinas, not three. The soul of consciousness, centered in the victim's head and throat and residing in his saliva can only be captured as he is dying by breathing his last breath."

The giant shifted resignedly. "To be affective, your victim should be literally scared to death. He must feel the horror of your evil as his heart bursts while you place your mouth over his and inhale his last breath."

Sakonige involuntarily let out a muffled shriek and covered her face. Ugidahli shivered at the cruelty the witch pleasured in.

The witch smiled proudly at his effect on the two naïve children. "The rest you know. Consume the other three askinas as you would of the raven. Whatever life the victim would have had is now yours."

As the gasping cannibal clutched his chest and laid back, Ugidahli was breathing heavily, his heart was racing, his stomach curdled, "The conjure. … What is the conjure?" he insisted.

Again Nunyunuwi laughed but was cut short by his rasping cough, "Yes, of course. The conjure."

The giant raised up and glared into Ugidahli's eyes with menacing, evil eyes and imprecated the curse in a maniacal, devious cadence. It was laced with eloquence and with archaic language that moved Ugidahli in a way he had never felt. He was convinced it was authentic. The witch collapsed as he whispered the final line.

Ugidahli struggled to keep from plunging his knife into the heart of this vile, cruel, evil creature who embodied the very essence of wickedness. But, he had given his word.

Shaking and delirious, he stood and backed away as the giant vomited yellow bile mixed with blood as if it were a taunt while keeping his eyes on the horrified boy. Ugidahli reached back grasping Sakonige's trembling hand, and turned and raced from the evil lair.

She was the perfect candidate and he had the power to transfer her long life to his old friend—the one living person on earth that really loved him and cared about him.

Once beyond the grasp of the evil witch, Ugidahli dropped onto a boulder sitting atop the hill overlooking the river where he had watched Nunyunuwi destroy and burn his camp. Sakonige burrowed into him trembling and exhausted. He wrapped his arms around her and hugged her tightly. "We are safe here. He will not dare follow us."

"Why? What made him so weak?"

Ugidahli told her the story that he had learned from Nvwoti Atlisdodi Usdi about the witch's curse on Nunyunuwi.

"That was Stone Clad?"

Ugidahli cradled her closer. The girl pressed against her protector and sweetheart, clinging to him in silence. He breathed a sigh of relief. He counted his blessings. They had survived with the help of Nvwoti's secret. He had the love of his life by his side and had secured the secret to immortality for his mentors. Life was good.

His thoughts turned to his mentors. He wondered how Adawehi and Ajilusgi were faring. "We must go now."

As the couple neared the home of the boy's mentors, his anticipation overcame him. He grabbed his sweetheart's hand and began to run through the forest. She pulled back, "Ugi. I can't do this, I'm exhausted."

Ugi tried to pull her after him, but she resisted more fervently, "You go on without me. I'll be right behind you."

He let go and sprinted off down the path. The familiar heptagonal house appeared sitting quietly beyond the rushing stream. He crashed through the stream and bounded into the house, "Ajilusgi. Adawehi. I'm back. I've got it. I've brought back the secret!"

Illuminated by the orange glow of the burning coals, Ugi could see his old friend lying by the hearth wrapped in a thick blanket. The dark silhouette of Ajilusgi lay on her bed. He ran to her.

"Grandmother. I've learned the secret. Just hang on and soon you will be well again."

The old woman did not stir. He grabbed her stiff shoulders to shake her, "Ajilusgi. Wake up, grandmother."

A tired, raspy voice called to him from the hearth, "She seeks her place in the afterworld. Speaking her name will call her back from her journey …"

Ugi knelt beside the sobbing old man, "Grandmother is …"

The old man's pained face told the boy that the old woman he loved and had risked his life to save had passed.

"Ugi?" Sakonige's tentative voice called from outside.

Ugi managed a timorous response, "In here."

Ugi was overcome by the tragedy. The sweet great aunt that had showed tenderness and understanding for him when no one else would have him was gone. And now the kindly old man who had taken him in and shared his knowledge and experience with him was near death. After all he had risked; after all he had given; he was faced with the real prospect that he had not and could not do enough.

Sakonige knelt next to her sobbing love and touched his shoulder, "Is everything alright, Ugi?"

Ugi sucked in his sobs long enough to explain, "Aji—Grandmother ... has passed. I am too late."

She hugged the agonizing boy warmly. The old man whispered softly, "Who is this, Ugi?"

Ugi straightened and sucked in a deep breath, "I apologize for my rudeness, Grandfather ..."

He took another deep breath, but the unfamiliar girl interceded, "I am Tlvdatsi Sakonige of the Ani Gilohi. My mother is Tlvdatsi Aji and my father is Waya Gani."

The tired old man smiled and then looked at his apprentice for an explanation. "It's a long story, Grandfather."

The old wizard nodded slightly, looked back at the girl and studied her for a moment before closing his eyes. Ugi sensed he was satisfied with the answer and had made his own assumptions. "I am Adawehi, Ani Wodi." He shared breathlessly.

Sakonige pushed in closer and placed her hand across his forehead, "Oh, Ugi, he's burning up with fever."

She sat back and loosened her cloth waist belt, unwrapped it and handed it to him, "Go to the stream and soak it for me."

Confounded by the girl's boldness, he hesitated. She placed her hand on his shoulder, "Go on, Ugi, the cold cloth will feel good on his feverish face."

The brash girl turned back to the dying man and caressed his face. Ugi resented her accepting attitude. He had not faced the monster so that he could return and make his mentor's death more comfortable. He unconsciously gripped one end of the waist cloth and wrapped it around his fist. She was young and healthy and had a long life ahead of her. She was the perfect candidate and he had the power to transfer her long life to his old friend—the one living person on earth that really loved him and cared about him. If not for the accidental potion, this arrogant girl would have nothing to do with him.

He visualized the strangulation and wrestled with how to manipulate her so that the old man could accept her last breath …

His victim turned to him and melted his resolve with her huge, dark, loving eyes and trusting smile, "Ugi?"

Shocked and embarrassed, he jumped to his feet and fled from the room. His heart was pounding and his mind spinning as he collapsed into the stream, buried the long waist cloth in the rushing waters and squeezed his eyes shut to block out the evil impulses that had momentarily seized him. He pulled the frigid, soaking cloth to his face and muffled his agonizing outcry. He held the soothing, cold cloth on his face as he tried to regain his sanity.

"Sakonige." A distant, singing voice called her name. He placed the cloth over his ears and tried to block it from his mind.

In a different pitch, "Sakonige."

"Sakonige." A different voice, still, from a different direction.

He realized that the voices were not from inside his head, they were real and from somewhere in the forest.

He pulled the dripping cloth from his ears and listened intensely.

"Sakonige." This time from close by. It had to be a search party. They were looking for the missing Sakonige.

Quietly, the guilty kidnapper sneaked out of the stream and headed in the direction of the voice. From tree to tree, he carefully shielded his approach and stealthily searched for the owner of the voice.

"Sakonige." The voice had to be no more than ten paces away. Ugidahli flattened his back against the tree and listened. The footsteps were coming his way. They stopped, shuffled and then were still. He could hear the russling sound of cloth and deep breathing. There was dead silence and then the sound of water splattering on the forest ground.

He cautiously peeked around the tree. In the dim, dusklike light, a tall, muscular man was standing with his back to him peeing into the bushes only a few paces away. Ugidahli pulled back quickly. His hands reminded him that he was still holding the damp waist cloth. His heart reminded him that his mentor was still dying back by the hearth. His imagination showed him the plan. Ugidahli watched it unfold in his head. He could see himself slipping up to the unsuspecting victim; wrapping the long cloth around his throat; tying it off and poking a short branch between the cloth and neck and twisting ... and twisting. He told himself that it would be easy with a stranger.

The trance was interrupted by the very real feeling of a strong man struggling. Startled to find himself gripping the short handle of the garrote with one hand and his other arm wrapped around the struggling man's chest, instinct compelled him to hang on as he was flung around and then slammed into a tree. He twisted the garrote handle tighter as the gasping victim tried to flip him over his head only to be dragged over with him. They writhed and rolled and wriggled on the pine laden forest floor.

Crazed and desperate, Ugidahli applied more and more pressure as the struggling man was kicking and fighting on top of him. How long could this man survive? Ugidahli cursed the stubborn man for his obstinate refusal to succumb.

The difficult victim rolled right, kicked back to the left digging and tugging with his fingers at the ever tightening cloth around his neck. Desperate fingers reached back, grabbed Ugidahli's hair and pulled as if hanging on to his last hope. Slowly the struggling man's efforts were replaced by jerking seizures. Ugidahli felt that he was riding a galloping elk. A limp hand released Ugidahli's hair. The seizures ceased.

Gasping for breath himself, he tightened his grip and hung on relentlessly. The bleached out world began to materialize around him. His senses began to return and his consciousness stepped in to assess his situation. The heavy body lying on top of him was limp. He was dead. He threw off the murdered man and rolled over onto his stomach in disbelief. He buried his face in the soft dirt and covered his head with his murderous hands.

Adawehi. He pushed up on his hands and knees. Numb from the realization of his actions, he impulsively crawled to the lifeless body and checked the reality of his death once more. Focusing on the urgency of his mission—to save his mentor—he pulled the body onto his shoulders and headed back to the hut.

Thou hast changed her mind with the new memories and made them pleasing. Ha!

WHEN HE BURST INTO the dark room, he could hear the soft sobs of Sakonige. The fire in the hearth was now only glowing embers. Ugidahli staggered across the room and dropped his hideous prize alongside his mentor.

"Adawehi. Wake up, you have to concentrate on what I tell you."

Sakonige's hand gripped his shoulder, "Ugi." She sniveled lovingly.

The driven apprentice ignored her, "Come on, Adawehi, we only have one shot at this."

"Ugi, he's passed."

Ugi turned his crazed face to her, "What?"

The sobbing girl's painful, grieving eyes told him, but he could not accept it. He grabbed the cold shoulders of his mentor and shook the dead man vigorously, "Adawehi. Wake up. I can save you now. Don't you understand? I can save you now."

From behind the urgent voice of Sakonige cried out, "Ugi, what is that?"

"Please, Adawehi, please wake up. I can save you now."

She persisted, "Ugi. What is this? What did you bring back?"

"No." he screamed as he fought off her attempts to gain his attention.

She grabbed his shoulders, "Ugi. Snap out of it."

He back-handed her knocking her on her side. She lay quiet and motionless. His frantic rage ceased, "Sakonige?" He questioned meekly.

Her heartbroken, muffled sobbing was barely perceptible. Relieved to hear her breathing, but sorrowful for his action, he grabbed her up and hugged her desperately. Her heart was possessed by him, so she had no choice but to forgive and accept him.

But as he held her tightly, his thoughts turned to the corpse of the searcher and the search party still in the woods. He pushed her back and stared earnestly into her eyes, "They have come for you. You must go back."

As she involuntarily sniggered, she wiped her eyes and tried to focus. He repeated, "The village has missed you and they are looking for you. You must go back now."

She understood what he was saying but did not understand this strange, cold person squeezing her arms and dispassionately wanting to send her away.

The cold, unemotional stranger stood and pulled her up with him. "You must not mention what you have seen nor where you have been. Do you understand?"

"No, Ugi, I don't understand. What has come over you?"

Unmoved by her impassioned plea, he distractedly mumbled to himself, "A potion. I need a potion."

After examining several pots in a frenzy, he turned to her perplexed. *I need a potion to take away her memory. I need to give her a new memory somehow. But there is nothing. This, they did not teach me.*

In the distance, he heard the searcher's calls. He could see that she heard it, too. He rushed to her, "Can I trust you?"

She was confused, but under the spell, she was bound to be faithful to him, "Of course, Ugi."

He led the obsessed girl down to the stream to the calm waters held back by the beaver dams where Adawehi had taught him how to transform into a raven with help from the seven boys. He led her to the middle of the pond. He hoped he could improvise on a conjure Adawehi had taught him for taking away bad dreams. Perhaps it could, with proper modifications, have the same effect on memories.

Facing her he imprecated, "Sge. She, who is of the Ani Gilohi is known to you as Tlvdatsi Sakonige. Where are you who apportions evil?"

The stunned girl frowned at her love. She seemed resigned to his whims, but confused.

"Ha. Now then, thou hast come to listen, Brown Beaver. He has apportioned evil for her. But now it has been taken, she is called Tlvdatsi Sakonige. The evil has been taken away from her mind. Yonder where there is a crowd that comes to apportion evil. She is Tlvdatsi Sakonige and her memories have become released. Her mind has been lifted up and changed. Her memories have been lifted up."

The witch motioned for her to submerge and then to scoop up a handful of water and rub it over her head, face and chest as he held the agate stones of his necklace in his fingers waiting for a reply from the spirits. If he felt movement in the white agate, the spirit had accepted his conjure. Movement in the black stone was rejection.

He felt nothing, so he continued, "Now then. Thou White Beaver at the headwaters of the stream. Quickly thou hast joined us. The evil memories have been taken from her and thou hast placed them beyond where they mean nothing anymore. Where no one cares what happens to them."

The white stone quivered ever so slightly. Ugidahli opened his eyes excitedly. Together they submerged and then Ugidahli scooped up a handful of water and rubbed it on his head, face and chest and then transferred the water impregnated with fabricated new memories to her head, face, and heart.

"Thou hast changed her mind with the new memories and made them pleasing. Ha."

He then led her out the other side of the pond. As they emerged, he saw the dreadful memories he had implanted of attempted abduction by Stone Clad and miraculous rescue changing her happy face to one of horror, torment, and fear. He felt her body tremble from replaced memories of how close to death she had come at the hands of the evil monster. Ugidahli slipped away as the search party converged on her.

"The monster," she shrieked as she pointed into the forest.

"Sakonige, are you alright?"

"He saved me!" She mournfully informed them, "He rescued me from the monster."

"Who rescued you, Sakonige?"

"That man … stranger …" with that, she collapsed into a protective deep sleep.

His eyes! Ugidahli dropped the pipe, gasped and scrambled back. The eyes of the corpse were open and focused on him. He shivered and jumped to his feet to study the corpse.

U GIDAHLI STOOD AT THE lonely doorway of the heptagonal house. A painful tingling rippled through his body leaving him with frightening images of the three corpses waiting for him. Dread overwhelmed him leaving him unmotivated to do anything. Sadly, he dragged himself to the hearth. He absent-mindedly placed logs over the coals and stirred the embers to ignite a flame. Adawehi's pipe caught his eye.

Gathering up the tobacco pouch and pipe, he sat where he had spent so many wonderful evenings with his dear friends. He pinched tobacco out of the pouch and stuffed it into the pipe bowl as he had watched Adawehi do so many times. He tamped down the tobacco, lit a splint with the growing hearth fire and held it over the bowl. The tobacco had never tasted so sweet; the smoke had never felt so warm in his lungs.

Tears streamed down his cheeks as he blew his message of mourning into the smoke of the hearth to be carried into the sky to notify the spirits that Ajilusgi and Adawehi would no longer be calling to them from center world. He prayed to the spirits to guide them to their place in the afterworld.

As the flames in the hearth began to rise up to consume the logs, orange and yellow light danced on the lifeless face of the stranger from the search party. His eyes! Ugidahli dropped the pipe, gasped and scrambled back. The eyes of the corpse were open and focused on him. He shivered and jumped to his feet to study the corpse.

"Uncle?"

Could it be? Ugidahli jumped over the hearth to roll the dead body onto its back. He straddled the familiar frame and looked into the familiar face. It was his hated uncle Awi-e Usdi.

Appalled, he reared back his head, lifted his fists to the heavens and threw all of his energy, agony, grief, and remorse into his blood-curdling scream. Willing the scream to cleanse his pain and his sins, he held it and forced it until his lungs failed and the world around him spun into a blurred, dizzying vortex. Drunk from his unfulfilled rage, deluded by his failed crusade to save his mentors, he felt alone in the world with nowhere to turn. His heart stung like a festering sore. His mind reeled in the morass of incomprehensible and intolerable misfortune. Nothing in his life had or could have prepared him for this outrageous predicament devoid of just conclusion.

How does the mind cope when overwhelmed by an impossible and unresolvable quandary? It is driven to resolution. It is the mind's purpose. And if the solution is determined to be madness, then that is the framework within which the mind must act. Because act it must! He felt the flush of his paradigm shift. A peaceful calm fell over him.

Ugidahli Unega faced his fate with a vindictive fervor and with steely calm and resolve, the happenstance witch began to loudly chant the conjure he had purloined from the cannibal witch as he fell upon his murdered uncle. Momentarily interrupting the conjure, he brutally released the waist cloth tourniquet around his victim's neck and sucked the bottled up and preserved last breath escaping from collapsing lungs.

Repulsed by his uncle's accusing stare, he drew his knife and surgically removed the hideous face as he continued the conjure. Placing the thin sheet of bloody skin over his own face, he plunged his knife into the chest penetrating the sternum and then cracked it open with a violent twist of the blade.

With the chest gapping, he pushed his fingers through and violently snapped it apart to expose the heart. He ripped it out ignoring the squirting blood spraying his face and ate it ravenously while continuing the archaic conjure spitting bloody droplets and bits of cardiac muscle.

Swallowing hard, he tossed the remainder of the heart into the fire as he reached in to pull out the liver. Dripping bile through his fingers, he bit a gapping plug out of it, tossing the surplus aside while he snapped a rib bone loose and sucked the juicy morrow out.

Triumphantly, he raised his bloody arms holding up the rib bone to the spirit world and finished the eloquent ending to the poetic imprecation.

His stomach convulsed, his muscles spasmed, his skin tingled, his eyes bulged, his tongue swelled as he catapulted off the gory feast and hurled himself into the wall and then tumbled to the floor writhing in pain. "If I die, so be it," he roared.

He rolled and tumbled and screamed and pounded his fist against the floor—his metaphor for all the injustices and betrayals in his life.

Then, as if all of the elements congealed, he felt a wonderful surge of energy and power fill his body followed by a euphoric sense of calm. He unfolded and blissfully stretched out across the floor on his back.

The ultra-juvenated witch rose up invincible. Effortlessly, he scooped up the mutilated corpse of his uncle and marched out of the house to the stream. Carelessly tossing the body across the stream, he plunged into the rushing waters and bathed exuberantly. Refreshed and cleansed he slogged out of the stream and picked up the body to continue to the forest where he intended to bury the evidence of his brutal feast.

"Ugidahli?" Before him stood his stunned uncle, the brother of the corpse in his arms who was quickly joined by two men Ugidahli assumed were also part of the search party.

"Is that …?" his uncle stared at his lifeless, faceless, mutilated brother. Ugidahli followed his uncle's eyes to look upon his incriminating evidence. Undeterred, the emboldened witch proclaimed, "It is Awi-e Usdi, Uncle. He has been ravaged by the cannibal."

He carefully laid the corpse on the ground amidst the gasping, horrified men. Overcome by grief, the corpse's brother fell down on his sibling and clutched his skinless face. His companions stood frozen with shock.

Ugidahli calmly commanded, "Go build a carrier."

The two obedient men trotted off grateful to distance themselves from the gory scene in front of them.

The emboldened witch placed his hand on his grieving uncle's shoulder. The devastated man turned and stared up at his nephew with flowing tears in his eyes. Wiping his face with both hands, the surviving uncle stood slowly, "And you, Ugi, where have you been … how are you?"

Ugi's face was hot and his pulse elevated. "I was captured by Nunyunuwi, but I managed to escape." He turned to his mutilated uncle, "Uncle was not so lucky."

His living uncle hugged the boy he thought he knew, "We are so happy that you are alive. We must get you home right away. Ganvnvi has been beside herself worrying about you."

The thought of returning to the village, of seeing his mother, of returning to a "normal" life, repulsed him. That life seemed like a million years ago. That timid, neglected boy seemed like someone else; someone he had known a million years ago. But, now, he was someone else entirely.

"I … can … not … return with you, Uncle."

His uncle frowned and waited for his explanation. What could he tell him? His mind was racing, searching for an excuse. "I have to stay and … bury my friends."

His Uncle looked behind his nephew, "There are others?"

Others? Yes, that was it. "Yes, Uncle."

"We will help you bury your friends, Ugi."

Ugi placed his hand on his uncle's chest, "No."

His uncle glared at him. Ugi backed off, caught his breath and regrouped, "You should take Uncle Awi-e Usdi back. I can bury my friends. They are not from the village and not your concern. And it is something I prefer to do alone."

His uncle looked back again and then at his nephew. "Nunyunuwi?"

Ugidahli glanced back, then at his mutilated uncle, then calmly into his uncle's eyes, "He has a full stomach. He will not be back soon."

His uncle looked back once more, then acknowledged with one quick nod before turning to kneel beside his brother. His two partners slipped up beside the carcass with a hastily constructed carrier. They gently placed the body of Awi-e Usdi onto the carrier and paused to give the grieving brother time. The poor man stood, turned and walked away as the carrier was lifted by the two nervous bystanders who solemnly followed their colleague.

Ugidahli Unega smiled wryly to himself.

There were the bones of others, but I was the only one not already butchered.

U GIDAHLI PAUSED AT THE edge of the clearing to look at the lodge pole walls lining the boundaries of the village. Around him birds chirped, the wind whispered through the trees, the water in the stream chattered as it splashed against obstinate stones dividing it and hummed as it reunited, flies buzzed in the edges of the warm sunlight, and flowers extended their fragrant welcome to the bees. He couldn't help but wonder why anyone would want to live in the stuffy confines of a fortress instead of in the free, open, fresh outdoors.

He had had a restless night. He didn't want to return to the village, but he wrestled with the fact that if he didn't, the village would come looking for him. He had concluded that to be truly free, he must confront his mother and family. As he approached the village, he realized that the children who would normally be laughing and playing by the stream were absent. As he approached the entrance, he noticed that the guard towers were manned. Fear of an attack by Nunyunuwi no doubt.

As he entered the "U"-shaped switch back entrance, a guard challenged him, but before Ugidahli could respond, the guard's colleague must have recognized him and waved him in. He heard the guard announce his name as he stepped out of the switch-back and entered the compound. Residents stepped out of their houses to stare at him and crowds began to gather around him as he approached his aunt's house. It was annoying and he frowned at them as he passed by. Above the clatter of the crowd, he could hear his mother's self-indulgent wails of mourning.

A small congregation marched purposefully up to him. He recognized the Uku, several he recognized as the elders who had examined his disfigured father including the baby-faced man who seemed to hang around with the elders. There were several other old men he had not seen before that he assumed were other clan elders. He also did not know the regally dressed person leading the procession. He speculated that he must be a Chief. The tall, stately man addressed him, "Ugidahli Unega."

Ugidahli did not respond. The chief continued, "We welcome you home."

Ugidahli remained silent as he suspiciously examined the forced smiles of several of the solemn men. "May we council with you?"

The Chief held out his hand inviting Ugidahli to walk with him. He looked beyond the contingent at his aunt's house only a few paces away. He hesitated before he reluctantly obliged. They walked side-by-side in silence down the narrow street and then turned onto the broad village avenue that led to the Council House. The Chief turned to the boy and smiled as they walked, "We were relieved to hear that you are alive."

Ugidahli continued to stare straight ahead, ignoring the Chief's attempts at civility and small talk. Well, not so much ignoring, in fact, not recognizing or understanding the practice. He had never seen, let alone spoken to a chief or anyone of rank other than his chance meeting with the Uku a lifetime ago. And his mind was still on his mission to confront his family. This was merely a diversion from his mission.

As they walked silently toward the Council House, Ugidahli drew strength from the powerful secret he held within. He was comforted by their naivete. He smiled at the thought that he was not the boy they thought they knew. He was not the innocent forest child they believed him to be. Even he marveled at the change he had experienced since he had last lived in this village so foreign to him now.

The Chief led the procession up the seven steps to the top of the mound where the large Council House stood. Once inside, the Chief invited his guest to sit on a red bench encircling half way around the massive hearth next to the large red throne. The elders took up places on the semi-circular white benches outside the red benches while the Uku sat on a large white throne behind the Chief's red throne.

An elaborately dressed, scrawny old man appeared and busied himself with preparing a beautifully decorated, long-necked, stone pipe. He passed the lighted pipe to the chief who majestically took the pipe, inhaled authoritatively, enjoyed the tobacco, and then exhaled the smoke slowly. He looked around the room at each of the elders and then at the Uku. Then he turned to Ugidahli and spoke, "This village mourns the loss of its brothers—first your father and now your uncle."

The stoic Chief returned to the pipe. He shook his head sadly as he exhaled. The strong smell of the tobacco was not as sweet smelling as Adawehi's.

The elders and the Uku shook their heads and whispered, "Sge."

"We are grateful that our daughter, Tlvdatsi Sakonige, was saved from a most certain brutal death."

He drew on the pipe deeply and held the smoke as he seemed to be in deep thought. As he allowed the smoke to escape, he nodded his head as if agreeing with himself. The elders and Uku nodded their heads in agreement. Ugidahli looked down to hide his face lest it betray how humorous he found the old men to be.

The Chief continued, "We grieve for the friends that you lost."

All eyes trained on Ugidahli for a response. He looked at them tentatively. What did they want from him? He put on his most pitiful look and nodded.

The chief resumed smoking, "Your uncle has said that you were captured by Nunyunuwi but escaped?"

It was a question but the Chief held on to the pipe. Ugidahli did not answer. The Chief sucked on the pipe as if munching on a snack and then handed it to his scrawny assistant to refill.

"We know of no other who has escaped from Nunyunuwi. Tell us your story Ugidahli Unega. We are interested in learning as much about Nunyunuwi as you can tell us. We can learn much from you."

The skinny assistant handed the refreshed long-necked ceremonial pipe to Ugidahli. He snatched the pipe and found it to be heavier than he had expected. He sucked on it eagerly. The tobacco tasted bland and bitter and burned his lungs and throat. He regretted that he had not learned Adawehi's secret to making sweet tobacco if this is what normal tobacco tasted like. Unimpressed, he exhaled the inferior smoke.

He scanned the faces of the old men who were all giving him their undivided attention except for the young man who sat with his eyes closed and shoulders slumped down and resting on his pot belly for support. Surely, he wasn't actually sleeping?

Ugidahli was unaccustomed to being the center of attention. He puffed up slightly and began, "He lives in a cave far away to the northwest."

He tried the pipe again. The smoke didn't burn as much or maybe he was used to it. It was better than nothing. "He would've eaten me if I hadn't gotten away."

He inhaled another big gulp of the pipe. What else was there to tell them? He wasn't going to share with them the giant's weakness. He wasn't going to tell them about his tiny Yunwi Tsunsdi friend who helped him escape. He handed the pipe back to the assistant.

Some of the elders looked about nervously. They turned to the one who appeared to be sleeping. Ugidahli grinned thinking that the impertinent man was about to get scolded. Suddenly, the apparently sleeping man's eyes popped open. Ugidahli almost fell off the back of his bench. The elders laughed at him as he squirmed forward on the bench to regain stability. The Chief directed the assistant to hand the pipe to "Sali."

Ugidahli remembered that "Sali" had been the one who postulated his father's demise as the work of a cannibal. Sali stared into nothingness apparently unaware or at least unconcerned that everyone was now staring at him. He accepted the pipe and curiously closed his eyes each time he sucked on the pipe. He was smacking and gulping and puffs of smoke billowed out the edges of his mouth. He couldn't be inhaling.

He laid the pipe in his lap and smacked his lips loudly for a moment. Then he cut his beady eyes at Ugidahli startling him again to the amusement of the council.

"Does he always wear the stones?"

Ugidahli did not answer as the man with the chipmunk face stared at him queerly. The assistant shuffled nervously and pointed at the pipe in Sali's lap. Sali either ignored him or just didn't notice him. The Chief intervened, "Sali, do you want the boy to answer?"

Sali cut his eyes to the Chief but did not move. The Chief directed the assistant who obediently whisked the pipe from Sali's lap and handed it to Ugidahli. Sali's eyes cut back to Ugidahli undeterred by his faux pas.

Ugidahli giggled at the strange man. He graciously took the pipe and imitated Sali's style of smoking as he glared back at him. A few of the elders quietly chuckled.

"He took them off in the cave. He piled them next to the entrance, stretched his arms and rubbed his shoulders where the straps had left deep imprints. Then he stretched out by the hearth, speared a heart lying in a pot next to him, held it over the fire for a few minutes and then ate it. All the while he stared at me like 'you're next'."

The elder's eyes grew large and they gasped. Ugidahli smiled proudly and handed the pipe back to the assistant. The assistant turned to Sali. Sali ignored him, "So, there was someone before you. Were there others?"

The assistant handed the pipe back to Ugidahli. He accepted the pipe but placed it in his lap, "There were the bones of others, but I was the only one not already butchered."

Sali followed up immediately, "Were there other ways into the cave besides the entrance?"

"There is now. I found a place where the ceiling had caved in blocking an entrance and removed enough to squeeze through."

Sali smiled, sat back, straightened his head and closed his eyes.

CHAPTER
33

Ugidahli left the Council House bewildered by what had just happened. He had come to the village to sever the ties with his family and with the village. Instead, he was now bound tighter. He had somehow been talked into leading the village warriors to Nunyunuwi. At the time, it had seemed very appealing to him—the idea of conquering the evil scourge. But now he thought that maybe it was a very bad idea. First of all, now what would he tell his mother? *Hi, Mom, I'm just here to help the village warriors kill the witch, Nunyunuwi, then I'm off to be a witch myself?*

And, after thinking about it, he doubted whether the warriors could conquer the monster anyway. He would be leading them to their death, most likely. But, of course, he couldn't very well share with them the secret curse that would defeat the evil witch. That would expose him as a witch.

What a mess he had gotten himself into. He really didn't want to be a witch, it had just happened. He really wanted to be a Kuni-Akati like he thought Adawehi and Ajilusgi were. But how could he do that now?

Ugidahli looked up to see that he was standing in front of his aunt's house. A flush of remorse flooded over him. He turned to flee.

"Ugi?"

He stopped. It was his aunt. "Siyo, Awinita."

He turned to find her flying into his arms. He had not counted on this. She hugged him tightly and warmly. Holding her young warm body against him reminded him of Sakonige. He wondered how she was faring. He had cursed her with dreadful memories. He hoped she was coping.

"Uncle told us about your capture! Are you ok?"

The deceitful nephew felt the pain of guilt grip him. "I am fine."

Awinita grabbed his hand and dragged him into the house, "Ganvnvi, look what I found!"

Ganvnvi was sitting by the hearth. She looked as if she had aged ten years. Her eyes were swollen, her cheeks were sunken, and streaks of gray hair dominated her stringy disheveled coiffure. Her sad eyes turned to her lost boy and teared as she reached out a trembling hand.

He froze. He couldn't force himself to accept her wretched hand. She attempted a smile but lost it in a painful grimace.

"Ugi! Go hug your poor mother. She has been worried to death."

Ugi's lower lip began to tremble, his chest felt cold and involuntarily trembled as well. He took a deep breath to summon his calm and resolve. His head felt faint as he tried to speak, "I did not come back to ..."

Ganvnvi folded her hands in her lap. She tilted her head back slightly, and trained stern eyes on her son, "What did you come back for my son?"

Ugi sobbed, "I'm not your son anymore!"

Ganvnvi and Awinita were stunned. Ugidahli already regretted his words, but stood with clenched fists trembling violently.

Awinita tried to hug him, but he moved away and stared cruelly at his mother. Ganvnvi turned away and stared at the low flames in the hearth, "Why would you say that to me?"

Ugidahli didn't answer. Ganvnvi rationalized, "You've decided to stay with Aji, haven't you? She has turned you against me."

It was Ugidahli's turn to be stunned. Why would she assume that? He felt compelled to defend his grandmother, "I have not been staying with Grandmother. Grandmother sent me away. … Only Ajilusgi would take me in. Only Ajilusgi loves me."

He could not stop the flood of emotion, "Now she is dead!"

He dropped to the floor and buried his head in his hands. Awinita fell on him, hugged him and sobbed with him.

When he looked up to his mother again, she was not sobbing. She was glowering hatefully into empty space. She spat her words in disgust, "Ajilusgi was a witch!"

Hate welled up in Ugidahli. He jumped to his feet, clenched his fists and lunged at his mother. The horror in her face stopped him. "I'd rather be a witch than live here!"

He stomped out of the house and ran madly toward the village entrance. Tonight he would seek refuge by the waterfall.

Ugidahli marched beside the Chief's lieutenant who was called Wahya. He was a tall, powerful, no nonsense man that reminded him of his father. He had decided almost instantly that he liked him.

As they topped the last hill before the stream marking the beginning of the place Adawehi had called the "Forbidden Forest", Ugidahli stopped and pointed toward a rugged, treeless outcropping of boulders in the distance. "His cave is up there."

Wahya halted the small army of warriors—all of the available warriors from the village. His eyes studied the outcropping and then surveyed the surroundings. He knelt, smoothed a spot on the ground and handed Ugidahli a short branch. "Draw me a map."

Ugidahli squatted over the smoothed ground and scratched out the basic layout of the mound of boulders indicating the cave and its two entrances. As he drew, Wahya continuously glanced at the mound and back to the drawing, asking Ugidahli where the places on the drawing were in fact on the mound. It made Ugidhali feel important and appreciated as he explained the relationship of his drawing to reality.

Wahya stood and scanned the terrain and then proclaimed, "We will camp in that grove of trees by the river tonight."

"He will see you," Ugidahli suggested matter-of-factly.

Wahya turned to him and frowned.

"That's where he captured me before."

Wahya looked back at his choice and scanned the area again. Without comment, he turned and walked back to look at the area from where they had come. "We will camp at that stream there."

He was pointing at a tributary that flowed into the river that bordered the Forbidden Forest but was blocked from view by the hill. He marched forth without consulting his guide. Ugidahli shrugged and followed the warriors back down the hill. He doubted that they would be safe even hidden by the hill.

While the warriors were getting their camp set up, Ugidahli disappeared upstream where he found a section of cascading water. He waded into the shallow rushing waters and pulled his crystal from his necklace, squatted, and held the crystal just beneath the flow. He called upon the spirits to show him the one of interest. Dancing images in the crystal congealed into a real-time image of Nunyunuwi resting peacefully in his cave next to the hearth.

As Ugidahli breathed a sigh of relief, the giant sat up, grabbed his stone cane, pointed it and stared menacingly at him through the crystal. As he had done before, he pulled the cane back to smell its tip and then laughed a great belly laugh. Ugidahli jumped up and backed out of the stream with alarm watching the image fade from the dripping crystal. He quickly replaced the crystal in his necklace and raced to warn Wahya.

The smell of freshly burning wood and the quiet rustling of men setting down their packs, raking the ground with branches, gathering firewood greeted Ugidahli as he searched for the towering leader. He found the Chief's lieutenant directing several men whose eyes were following his finger pointing to different points atop the hill sheltering them from view of Nunyunuwi's cave. Ugidahli's concern was growing. Posting guards would not work against the magic of the monster. He was convinced that Nunyunuwi already knew they were there and probably knew the layout of their camp.

The guards rushed off to take up their designated positions. As Wahya turned, Ugidahli interrupted him, "He knows we're here."

Wahya's brow furrowed as he paused before the boy. Ugidahli was intimidated by the imposing man's doubtful stare and before he realized what he was saying, blurted out, "I saw him in the crystals."

The tall man frowned and cocked his head to one side, "You saw him where?"

Beads of sweat appeared on Ugidhali's forehead as his face burned and his senses numbed. Now what could he say? His mind fumbled for a plausible explanation, but, of course, there was none. He sensed that Wahya was getting impatient. Would Wahya believe the truth?

"I ... uh ... I can read the crystal." He lifted the necklace to show Wahya the crystal in the netted pocket.

Wahya crossed his arms, breathed in deeply, reared back and glowered down on him. What he had said sounded crazy even to Ugidahli. He could feel his heart pounding in his ears. He realized that he had said too much already. Wahya shook his head and stomped off. Ugidahli kicked the sand. *Fine!* He consoled himself, *but you'll be sorry you didn't listen to me.*

The darkness of the night was profound, the fires in the several campfires had burned down to glowing embers, warriors were snoring loudly like creek frogs when a scream rang out from one of the guard posts at the top of the hill. Ugidahli saw Wahya and several warriors bound up the hill and joined in behind them. They were unprepared for what they found at the guard post. The replacement guard was cowering near the mutilated body of the guard he had come to replace.

Wahya dropped to the side of the gruesome corpse, "Nunyunuwi!"

A raucous noise bellowed from the camp site, cries of pain, clashing of stone on stone, yelling, the tell-tale signs of a furious battle. Wahya drew his war club and bounded back down the hill followed closely by his small contingent. Ugidahli hesitated. He was brushed aside by the replacement guard scrambling to catch up with the others. Ugidahli knew that they would be too late. His fears were confirmed by the deafening silence that settled over the valley below. Not even crickets stirred.

When Ugidahli finally garnered the courage to return to camp, he was not surprised by what he found. Bloody, hacked up bodies were strewn around the camp, war clubs littered the ground, wounded warriors were helping each other assemble for the Kuni-Akati to look at them. Wahya and his contingent were busy comforting the wounded, interviewing them, and surveying the carnage.

Ugidahli found a stump to sit on to watch and study the battlefield. The crumpled bodies formed a wake defining the path of the monster. He imagined the giant with his stone armor racing in from the west hacking and clubbing the groggy warriors futilely trying to defend themselves. Many dead before they even understood what was happening to them. The wounded being interrogated pointed to the east where Nunyunuwi had undoubtedly fled after demolishing the camp. Ugidahli warily studied the eastern end of the camp wondering if the demented monster was gloating at his triumph from the darkness. Was he waiting to come back through and finish off the powerless survivors?

He wanted to consult his crystals, but he doubted that the campfires of the spirits in the sky would provide enough light to discern images. Instead, he clutched the stones and asked the spirits if Nunyunuwi would attack again. As if answering his plea, a monstrous roar announced the return of the stone clad giant.

Ugidahli dove into the bushes to hide and listen to the anguished cries of brave men being pummeled by the death blows of Nunyunuwi's war club and ax. The horror lasted only moments before total silence returned. The hiding boy did not want to stir. He did not want to know what remained of the war party. Was Wahya dead as well?

The horrifying awakening struck him as he listened to the whimpering survivors struggling to reach out and to hang on to life. It hit him in a word—"Revenge!"

Nunyunuwi would no doubt go for the undefended village to seek revenge for the arrogant attack. Ugidahli jumped to his feet. *Sakonige!* Only he could save the village from the cruel, vengeful attack. Only he knew the monster's weakness. There was no time to waste, he began the chant even as he approached the stream.

The fiery raven-witch streaked across the dark sky unnoticed and alighted on the thick branch of the huge oak crowding the north wall of the village. How would he do this? He was certain that the villagers would not respond to his summons. His only recourse was to appeal to the Uku. He launched off the branch and glided through the door of the Uku's small hut startling the old man sitting solemnly next to his hearth. The Uku gasped and began to mutter a protective prayer. Ugidahli shape-shifted back into human form and paused to let his mystical entrance soak in.

"Ugidahli?" The old Uku muttered in disbelief.

Ugidahli employed his most sincere and authoritative demeanor, "Grandfather, forgive me for startling you, but there is no time for traditional cordialities. Nunyunuwi has conquered and vanquished the valiant war party from our village. Now, he is on his way to destroy the people of the village. Women and children and elderly will be no match for him. He will easily kill them all."

The Uku was gasping for breath and blinking his eyes wildly trying to comprehend. "We must hide! We must round up everyone and flee!"

"He will find you? There is no time! I know the witch's weakness and we can defeat him, but I will need your help and we must not hesitate."

The Uku did not appear to be convinced, "I will consult the stones."

Ugidahli's stomach churned. "Hurry, Uku, we are in grave danger."

The Uku reached into his pouch and pulled out the stones with his trembling hands, held them in his palms with his thumbs resting on them, closed his eyes and mumbled his query. When the white stone squirted out of his hand landing in the flames of the hearth, the Uku was convinced!

Ugidahli fished the stone from the flames with a log as he explained the plan. Having heard old men tell stories at ceremonial feasts his mother had dragged him to when he was little, he tried to imitate their style to lend credence to his story.

"This is what was told to me by the … wise one. Many, many years ago, before anyone alive today remembers, Nunyunuwi made the mistake of capturing what he supposed to be a pretty young virgin. After ravaging her and as he was strangling her, the witch dropped her façade. The stunned rapist staggered away and purged his stomach. The triumphant witch cackled and taunted the repulsed assailant and placed a curse on him."

Ugidahli paused as he remembered his mischievous little friend taunting him when he told the story. He smiled and finished, "From that day forward, Nunyunuwi loses all of his strength and powers in the presence of a menstruating virgin."

The Uku did not respond. He seemed distant and disoriented. Ugidahli stood and commanded, "Gather up seven menstruating virgins and bring them to me and then …"

The Uku stood and with quivering voice muttered as he scurried out of the hut, "I must go to the elders!"

"No, you old fool. There's no time for council. Nunyunuwi is coming. Don't you get it?"

As the old man gave his best impression of running, he yelled at the top of his lungs, "Elders! Chief! Nunyunuwi is coming! Elders, warriors, chiefs assemble!"

Ugidahli was confounded by the Uku's totally un-expected actions. He didn't know whether to race after the crazy old man and tackle him, race off to the village exit and leave these petty imbeciles to fend for themselves, or go to the council and plead his case. The second option was most appealing, but he could not desert Sakonige.

The crazed Uku scaled the seven steps to the Council House with amazing agility and disappeared inside. Villagers had poured into the streets to check out the commotion. They made way for the elders as they galloped to the Council House. Dozens pounded on the door of the War Chief to roust him out. Soon the whole village had gathered around the Council House.

Ugidahli stood in amazement at the spectacle. It had only taken a couple dozen heartbeats to assemble the entire village. He chuckled and shook his head. Maybe this was better yet.

Seeing Ugidahli calmly pushing inside hushed the noisy, unruly assembly. He found the Uku kneeling and pleading with the confused War Chief standing at his throne. The elders were crowded around them all talking at once. When the Chief spotted Ugidahli, he looked shocked and then raised his hands to settle the room. The Uku turned to see Ugidahli and then shrunk back against the legs of the astonished elders.

"You have returned?"

A rumble of muffled conversations rolled around the Elders until the Chief spoke again.

"Do you bring news?"

Ugidahli calmly strolled through the center of the Council House and stood opposite the hearth from the Chief. "I regret that I do not bring the news you wait for. Nunyunuwi has vanquished the war party and is now on his way here to affect his revenge on the village."

The assembly collectively gasped. Outside, the news raced through the crowd and the wails of the women permeated the thick walls of the Council House. The Chief glanced about nervously. The elders were speechless. The Uku was gripping his heart and gulping for breath.

"We must not panic, Chief, for I bring good news."

All eyes trained on the speaker, "I know Nunyunuwi's weakness. We can defeat him."

Random noise consumed the Elders once more. The Chief raised his arms for quiet. The Uku glared at Ugidahli. Ugidahli focused on the Uku. "Many years ago a great witch put a curse on the man of stone. He will lose his power in the presence of a menstruating virgin. We must assemble seven virgins in their time and place them in his path."

The Chief and the elders turned to the Uku and argued among themselves. Miraculously out of the chaos the soft words of the young, baby-faced man quieted the room, "I have heard that."

All eyes trained on Sali who had been sitting quietly with his eyes closed in his usual spot on the circular white bench. The Chief rushed over to the chubby man, "What did you say, Sali?"

Sali's eyes popped open and cut to Ugidahli. "It's an ancient myth. What proof do you have?"

The room turned to Ugidahli. Challenging eyes focused on the messenger. Ugidahli was on the spot. Under pressure he fabricated an argument, "Why do you think the great monster allowed Sakonige to go free?"

The Chief challenged him, "She was rescued by your uncle, was she not?"

"He could have swatted him away like a fly if he had wanted to. But he didn't. Instead of a tasty virgin, he settled for a gristly old man."

Sali pulled back and closed his eyes, "What he says makes sense."

The Chief and the Elders studied the younger man and then turned to the Uku. The old priest had regained his composure and stood confidently keeping his eye on Ugidahli. This was the moment of truth. Would the Uku choose to betray him or allay his secret and save the village. The Uku moved forward and turned to the chief, "We must have seven virgins in their time step forward. Each clan should participate!"

He strolled outside to address the grieving crowd followed by the clan elders. He challenged members of each clan. To Ugidahli's amazement, seven unclean virgins were offered up.

Do not let his innocent demeanor deceive you for I have witnessed his dark magic myself. Seize Ugidahli Unega and cast him on the fire that he may burn with his kind and that we may be cleansed of his malefaction.

Ugidahli was both encouraged by the Uku's taking charge and worried. As the Uku positioned the unclean ones outside the village along the path leading in, the War Chief assembled volunteers for an ambush inside the village should the virgins fail. Meanwhile the Peace Chief took charge of evacuating the children and meek out the back entrance. Ganvnvi fashioned herself as a great helper in this cause.

And then, they were ready. It had come to the dreadful task of waiting for the monster to arrive. Ugidahli had been positioned in the sentinel alongside the other young boys with good archery skills. They would be the first to face the man of stone if he got past the virgins. The Chief had positioned the rest of the archers left in the village to hide on the roofs of the houses just inside the compound. These were mostly young boys too young to be included in the war party.

The hunters that were too old to have joined the war party but still capable of handling the bow and arrow were strategically placed behind cover of houses, asis or storage sheds. The women who had volunteered to stay and fight, which was almost all of the young girls and women who didn't have babies to care for were given long spears and hidden inside the houses.

Ugidahli watched patiently from the sentry tower as the War Chief marched around the village checking with everyone, reassuring them, building their spirits and confidence. He turned to gaze outside the village looking for signs of Nunyunuwi in the darkness. He feared that if the stone man didn't come soon, the Chief, Elders, and Uku might start getting anxious, even doubtful. A lot was resting on Nunyunuwi actually coming. What if he had decided not to attack the village? What if he had changed his mind and decided to go back to feast on the dead warriors instead? Why not? There were enough carcasses to feast on for a long time back at the camp. Ugidahli was worried.

At first, he thought it was a panther growling in the distance. He grew concerned that the great cat might foil the plan and go after one of the virgins waiting for Nunyunuwi. The boys around him in the guard tower stirred and glanced about as they readied their bows and arrows. But when he heard it again, there was no mistaking the distinctive roar. Nunyunuwi had arrived!

The third growl was deafening followed by a fourth. Each roar becoming weaker and weaker. Ugidahli bolted down the stairs of the guard tower and zig-zagged through the entrance switchback. As he exited the village entrance, he raced out to meet the monster as he staggered up the path. Encircled by the brave virgins, blood streamed from his mouth and nose. Ugidahli seized the weak man's stone cane and plunged its pointed end into the monster's chest. The monster raised his fist at Ugidahli and managed one final roar before collapsing on his back with a huge thud that blasted dust all around him and forced the virgins to turn away and place their hands over their faces to block the discharge.

The Uku appeared from the forest with his arms raised above his head gripping the long shaft of a sourwood spear. He scurried up to the defeated giant and plunged his spear into the giant's limp body. Six Elders poured out of the woods and impaled their sourwood spears, as well. The defeated monster accepted the spears without complaint.

Part of the chief's small militia was ordered to form a perimeter guard around the monster. The brave ones kicked and spit on the monster. All others were directed by the Uku to gather firewood to pile on him. Nunyunuwi began to plead with the Uku promising him great secrets if he would spare him. This perked up Ugidahli's ears. He went to the desperate witch and encouraged him to divulge some of his secrets. Nunyunuwi jeered at the young witch and replied, "What power do you have to save my life?"

Ugidahli argued, "It was I that convinced the village to rise up and defeat you."

Nunyunuwi studied the boy thoughtfully. "I don't believe you have the power to stop this."

"Very well." The boy turned nonchalantly and walked several paces away to sit down and stare at the knowledge-able witch, just in case his bluff worked.

All of the villagers, including the women, children, and old men, began to file by and dump their logs and sticks and trash on their conquered enemy. As the pile grew, their enemy began to plead more desperately with the Uku who stood detached as he directed the campaign and called upon the white spirits to remove his dark magic. The elders positioned themselves around the doomed witch much as they would around the dance field—by clan position. Ugidahli was unnerved when Sali strolled up and sat beside him. He had no idea where the deer clan should sit, nor did he know the Deer Clan Elder. It didn't matter to him, anyway, he wanted to be near the head of the wizard in case he uttered any conjures of interest. Sali sat in what Ugidahli had come to recognize as his usual manner, like a round ball with a round, pudgy head sleeping atop it.

Nunyunuwi defiantly held out until the Uku ordered a piece of the sacred fire be brought from the Council House. The representative burning coals were placed on top of the mound of firewood and encouraged to spread. Faced with the dire consequence of being incinerated, Nunyunuwi began to plead with all of the Elders and offered samples of the wondrous knowledge he could share with them. Ugidahli sucked up the morsels greedily as if feasting on fine morsels of venison.

The flames grew and the villagers reveled and danced around the bon-fire. Ugidahli focused on the desperate witch powerless to avert his fate. Nunyunuwi turned to him with desperate eyes. The two witches connected.

Nunyunuwi began to sing the sacred songs for hunting, for the sacred ceremonies, for the stages of life, for entreating game, for curing the different ailments that could be put under someone, for strength in times of peril, for comfort in times of hardship and the flames grew and the heat increased and the fire burned closer.

The omniscient witch imprecated conjures for all manner of sickness, pain, aches, desires, dreams, fate, love, and curses and Ugidahli drank them in like fresh water, but the fires crackled louder and stronger and spread as they consumed the breadth of the cone-shaped pile.

The heat beneath the fire must have been intense for the witch was sweating profusely, his skin glowing fire red and his eyes becoming more and more intense. His stone armor had become a stone oven heated by the flames. And the closer the fire burned down, the more intense his proliferation of knowledge. Even the onlookers and revelers pushed back from the scorching heat.

Ugidahli reveled in the enlightenment. The knowledge he had devoured from his mentors paled in comparison to the bounty of knowledge now being relinquished. This plethora of wisdom, revelation, insight, and interpretation expanding the ideologies, doctrines, traditions and expertise of medicine, philosophy, religion, and culture was almost overwhelming.

He was confident that he could now rescue mankind from its miseries and tribulations. Ugidahli envisioned the elders and Uku branching out across the Ani Yun Wiya, the real people, the Cherokee world and treating the weak, uplifting the down trodden and leading all mankind to the seventh level of achievement and self-fulfillment. Had only this dark witch turned to the white path and dedicated himself to the empowerment of man rather than the selfish passions of sin!

With the fire raging and the man of stone succumbing to the holocaust, the Uku took center stage at the head of Nunyunuwi and raised his hands in proclamation, "The dark way cannot coexist with the white way."

The revelers and onlookers hushed and engaged the Uku.

"Followers of the dark way must be purged."

The crowd cheered enthusiastically.

"There are no exceptions."

His audience shouted their agreement.

The Uku dropped his hands to his chest and changed his countenance to one of sincerity and concern, "We have in our midst one who has gone to the dark side."

Here and there a shout, but mostly attentive silence held the villagers waiting for their most revered resident to continue. Ugidahli's pulse began to rise. He did not like the way this was shaping up.

"The sacred fire now purges the dark witch that has cursed us for many years. But can we let darkness prevail beyond his demise? Can we rest on our laurels and turn a blind eye to the evil that remains among us?"

Wary eyes glanced about and a low rumble rose up in the crowd. What was he referring to? What did he mean? Ugidahli thought he knew.

"We cannot allow our hearts to jeopardize our lives. Think of your loved ones. Wherever we find the dark way, we must purge it. Do you not believe this?"

The believers shouted their agreement.

"Then believe what I must now tell you. A vile and accomplished tsigili is in our midst still eager to replace the monster before us."

The crowd gasped and listened intently.

"Do not let his innocent demeanor deceive you for I have witnessed his dark magic myself. Seize Ugidahli Unega and cast him on the fire that he may burn with his kind and that we may be cleansed of his malefaction."

The crowd gasped in awe, Ganvnvi gasped and then screamed, "No!"

Ugidahli stood and backed to the stream as the crowd cautiously approached. In the stream, he spread his arms and tilted his head back as he called upon the spirits and the seven boys. His eyes began to burn red, the skin on his face strained and deformed as black downy hairs sprouted. His nose and mouth shape-shifted into a beak as his arms and body feathered. The astonished crowd backed away in fear as the Uku challenged them to seize him.

A sparkling flame flashed around his body. Fiery sparks spewed from his arms and body as the tsigili jettisoned into the sky escaping this final betrayal.

He had never done anything on the dark side for himself, it had always been to help others. Now, with all the knowledge he had gleaned, think of the wondrous things he could do for the people.

Ugidahli Unega glided above the forest feeling sorry for himself. Nor did he understand why things had turned out so horribly for him. He had never had any malice toward anyone. Why hadn't his family loved him? Why hadn't he been close with his father the way he was with his father's family? His father had been aloof and independent but Ugi had never felt that his father didn't like him just that his father did not show emotion toward anyone—good or bad.

Ugidahli had always felt like a burden on his mother, someone who never shared a kind word with him. She had been so unhappy living in the woods away from the village that he had found it ultimately better to play alone in the woods than to be around her. And she had seemed to prefer it that way. His mother's family hated him. Well, his aunt Awinita had been nice to him. His father's family seemed to love and accept him, but had rejected him when he needed them most.

Sakonige only liked him because he was different or odd maybe. Without the potion, she just felt sorry for him and only had affection for that dumb boy she hung around with. He felt that if he ever released her from the potion, she would most likely hate him.

The only people in his life that had accepted him and made him feel loved were Adawehi and Ajilusgi. Of course, Ajilusgi was sort of family being his grandmother's sister, however, he wasn't sure that counted since she had been rejected by the family. But now they were dead.

And in spite of their love, he was now banished from the Cherokee people because of them. All he had intended to do was try to save them. And he had not gone down the dark path for himself. He had never done anything on the dark side for himself; it had always been to help others. Now, with all the knowledge he had gleaned, think of the wondrous things he could do for the people. And this was the thanks he got for it.

He looked down at the passing trees and realized that he was about to pass over the heptagonal house. He guessed he had subconsciously gravitated to it. He turned his wings and circled around to land at the once happy place. Maybe he could hold up here for the winter. There was corn, beans, and squash left in the storage hut. The asi would be warm on bitterly cold nights. No one would look for him here. He would be safe until he could find a better place and decide what he would do with the rest of his miserable life.

Udo tried to change the subject, "We heard about Stone Clad and the village thing. They call you …"
Udo said the name grandly, "Kalanu Akyeliski." He giggled, "That's your new name now."
Ugi chuckled with him, "Raven Mocker?"

Ugidahli awoke and felt chilled. He pulled his blanket snuggly around him and tried to go back to sleep. The light of morning had found its way into the heptagonal house but it was still and quiet outside. The usual chorus of birds and whispering trees was missing. Today he had planned to go hunting to replenish his meat supplies. He glanced at the door and could see light glistening below the bear-skin cover. He concentrated on it and realized that snow had filtered in on the floor. It was the first snow of winter.

"Oh, great. Snow."

His bladder ached but he didn't want to get up yet. He turned over and pulled the blanket over his head. Then he pulled it back again and checked the hearth. The embers had cooled. He didn't want to have to restart the fire from scratch, so he raised up and pulled the blanket around his shoulders as he tossed sticks and kindling over the embers and stirred them slowly while blowing softly and steadily. Thankfully, the embers ignited and the kindling soon began to crackle. He placed three logs over the kindling and then forced himself to step outside to relieve his bladder.

Surprisingly, it didn't feel that cold outside. There was no wind and the misty fog felt like a snowy blanket. Snow had a way of muffling all sounds. The sky was overcast so there were no shadows to inform him that Sister Sun was high in the sky. When he had finished, he turned to return home but stopped short.

Someone … something was standing under the porch by the door. At first, he thought it was a deer. "How convenient." He thought that before realizing his bow was inside. But, then the deer appeared to drop to its side and a stocky man stood up. Ugidahli stepped quietly to one side behind a large tree to watch the intruder. Perhaps, a hunter looking for shelter?

"Ugi?"

The voice was familiar. When the intruder turned to look around, Ugi recognized his uncle Udo. Udo increased the volume for his second inquiry, "Ugi? Are you here?"

Ugi hesitated. Did he want to see his uncle? Uncle Udo had always been a good friend to him. He remembered that afternoon sitting beside him tying arrowheads to shafts. It was one of the best days of his life.

"Udo?"

Ugi stepped out and his uncle smiled warmly and rushed up to hug him. It felt good to be hugged and Ugi hung on for a moment. When they broke apart, Udo slapped his nephew's shoulders and looked him over. "How are you, Nephew?"

Ugi shrugged. "What brings you here? How did you know …"

Udo laughed happily and punched Ugi's shoulder, "You thought you tricked me that day, didn't you?"

Udo nodded his head agreeing with himself, "You were pretty clever, but not as clever as Uncle Udo, eh?"

Ugi shook his head in disbelief, "You knew?"

"Of course I knew, Nephew."

An awkward moment of silence fell over them. Ugi was at a loss for words but his mind was pregnant with questions.

"Well, come inside and sit with me."

The two men made a big thing of rushing inside and pretending to be cold and pretending to be warmed by the anemic fire. Ugi added logs and encouraged the flame to consume them.

"How is Grandmother … and uncles?"

Udo's laughing eyes turned away and became sad. "She mourns for you, Ugi."

Ugi paused to try to understand and then busied himself again with the fire.

Udo glanced at his nephew and then continued, "She mourns for your soul. It made her sad when she learned you had turned to Ajilusgi. She blamed herself for sending you away."

"I didn't know Ajilusgi was …"

"That's what I told her, Ugi. You didn't know Ajilusgi was a witch."

Ugi looked up at his apologetic uncle, "I meant to say that I didn't know Ajilusgi was my aunt."

Udo's expression saddened again. Gravely he asked, "You knew she was a tsigili?"

Ugi quickly corrected him, "Oh, no … not at first. It's just that Adawehi and Ajilusgi were the only ones who … wanted me."

Udo cursed and spun around taking a swing at the air. "That's not true, Ugi. We wanted you, but …"

Udo turned back to his nephew and pleaded, "… well, you know, the clan thing."

Ugi shrugged. "It's the past. Nothing we can do about it now."

Ugi pulled out his old mentor's pipe and the last pouch of tobacco, "Let's smoke, Uncle, we have a lot talk about."

Ugi sat beside the hearth and motioned for his uncle to join him. Udo did so reluctantly.

"Why did you come today, Udo?"

Udo shifted, "When I saw Mother staring sadly out the door at the snow, I knew what she was thinking. So, I sneaked off to check on you."

Ugi blinked away a tear. His grandmother was worried about him. He couldn't really remember anyone worrying about him before, except maybe Adawehi or Ajilusgi when he left them to seek the monster. It hurt deeply knowing that she missed him, especially now that it was too late.

Udo tried to change the subject, "We heard about Stone Clad and the village thing. They call you …" Udo said the name grandly, "Kalanu Akyeliski." He giggled, "That's your new name now."

Ugi chuckled with him, "Raven Mocker?"

"Funny name, huh?"

Ugi shook his head, "I should never have exposed myself to the Uku."

Udo grew serious and studied his nephew. Ugi shrugged sheepishly. Udo put up his hands and pulled back, "Whoa, Nephew, that's creepy stuff. You're in deep, huh?"

Ugi snickered at his uncle's feigned fear. He tamped down the tobacco into the bowl of the pipe and lit a splint. He WAS in deep, maybe deeper than any person alive. He lit the pipe and inhaled the sweet blend of his mentor. As he exhaled the wonderful smoke, he declared, "I would trade all that I know about the dark ways for the recipe to make this tobacco."

He handed the pipe to his uncle who took it gingerly and examined it for a moment before placing it in his mouth and sucking on it. Immediately, his uncle fell into a coughing fit, gasping desperately for his breath. Ugi impulsively dipped a bowl in the pot of water next to the hearth and handed it to the gasping guest who gulped down the water frantically only provoking his choking lungs. Ugi grabbed his uncle's shoulder and pounded his back. In his most soothing voice, he whispered, "Relax, take a slow, deep breath, relax ..." just as Ajilusgi had done for him so long ago.

When Udo finally regained his breath, he explained, "We don't have tobacco up in the mountains."

"I'm sorry, Udo, I didn't think about that."

Udo shrugged. The two sat quietly. Udo sipped on the water and then handed the bowl to Ugi, "I'd better get back. Could snow more today."

Ugi transferred the bowl to the hearth and nodded sadly.

As they walked out of the house, Udo gestured toward the field dressed deer, "I brought you something to eat."

Ugi nodded, "Wado."

They continued down to the stream in silence. Udo smiled at his lonely nephew, "I will tell Mother you are keeping warm and have plenty to eat."

Ugi smiled and nodded. "Maybe I will drop in for a visit sometime."

A tear rolled down Udo's cheek. He looked down and stirred the snow with his foot, "You can't come visit, Ugi."

Ugi looked away, "I know."

Udo nodded and walked away without looking back at his nephew. Ugi watched his uncle lumber off into the misty forest until he disappeared in the fog. Tears gushed from his eyes as he dropped to his knees and pressed his head into the cold snow. He knew he could never see his family again.

Selu, corn, was the mother of man. She would save him. But his weak body would not respond. Dreams tried to push away his reason. Sweet dreams; so inviting. The world drifted away.

Winter dragged on for Ugidahli, or Kalanu Akyeliski, as he was now known. The name sounded like a mean old man. He didn't feel old or mean. He felt lonely and forgotten. His life had no meaning; he had no ambition; nothing to look forward to; nothing to be proud of.

It was clear that Ugidahli Unega was dead. Maybe it was time to go with the new name. He was a different person now. He was, no matter what his intention had been, a witch, a tsijili most vile. Society would not accept him as a wizard or medicine man, even though he could be one. What good was his voluminous knowledge if he could not use it; if no one cared about it; no one needed it; no one appreciated him? What did life offer to a Raven Mocker?

There were days when he didn't go out. There were times when he would sleep for days only waking to expel his bladder or sip on cold soup. He had come to sleep atop the rectangular slabs covering the tombs of Adawehi and Ajilusgi as a way to be near them; his only friends in his dismal life. The cold winter winds drove him inside and the dreary, overcast skies laid depression under him. The snow fell and the heptagonal house became increasingly inadequate. The inviting womb of the asi drew him in. Warmth would be easy in the small, dug-out pit house with its thick, domed roof.

The Raven Mocker dragged all of the hides and blankets into the small, domed pit. He piled the blankets high, crawled under them and drifted back into his depression-fed hibernation. He slept like a lonely bear in his cave waiting for spring. When the weather permitted; when his energy permitted; he would leave the cozy hut to replenish his food supplies. But the cold winds of winter or the debilitating power of his depression often left him too tired to start the fire; too tired to gather wood; too tired to replenish his food supply; too tired to care.

It must have been the middle of winter, Unolutani, the month of the Cold Moon. Sister Sun's light fingers reached through the smoke hole of the Asi to dance on his slumbering eyes. Rejoicing birds chattered outside and the room felt warm and inviting. He crawled out from under his mound of blankets and rolled onto his back. The crisp air felt invigorating.

"Enough," he declared. Raven Mocker sat up and started to place a pot of Three Sisters soup onto the embers, but there were only cold, black ashes in the hearth. He was hungry and weak, but on this day, his mind was strong. Munching on snow balls he busily gathered wood and started the fire, found corn, beans and squash in the decrepit corn bin and happily heated a well-needed breakfast. His stomach was empty and yet it still wanted to reject the warm soup. He leaned back against the earthen walls of the asi and ate slowly.

It was a day when the Raven Mocker had grown tired of his depression. His mind was actively planning. He would stock the Asi for the rest of winter. He would need lots of firewood. He would fix a big pot of soup. Venison and rabbit meat would be good. With the sun high, he could not waste time, he had to get busy.

His surge of energy and purpose lasted for three days before the scourge of winter returned with a vengeance and drove him back into the asi. The wind relentlessly howled around the cramped pit house and long, lonely days once again reminded him how worthless his life had become. It was as if his burst of optimism had made his depression that much worse by contrast. For a few days, he had soared to great heights of purpose and the industry of stocking his asi had pushed aside the dismal reality that his life had no purpose beyond self-preservation.

But the idle time refocused his mind on his reality. He became slovenly and lazy. He sank to new lows—sometimes urinating inside; sometimes eating raw venison; vomiting in a corner of the asi; lying sick and knowing the cure but too lazy to employ it; hoping he would die. Fever drove him to delirium. The days became a blur; his life became a blur; he dreamed horrid dreams he could not wake from; dreams that repeated over and over; dreams that told him he would soon die; he waited for death; he longed for death; he dreamed he was dead.

Kalanu Akyeliski awoke sweating. He looked around the dimly lit room. He was not freezing. He was not dead. There was no fire in the hearth, but the room seemed warm. Flies were swarming over the rotting carcass of the deer he had slain … he didn't know how long ago … the stench was sickening. They were buzzing around the pot that once held soup, also. His stomach felt so empty that it even craved the air he breathed.

He sat up and felt dizzy and weak and nauseous. He reached for the pot of soup. He would eat it cold as he had done so many times but when he placed the edge of the bowl to his lips, he pushed it away. The smell. He looked into the pot that was devoid of liquid but was crawling with fat white worms. He slung it across the room and gagged but his stomach was too empty to vomit.

Desperately, he crawled on his hands and knees to the door and pushed his head through the heavy bear-skin cover gasping for fresh air. Food, he had to eat something, anything, his stomach felt hollow.

The snow had retreated from the asi, but the brown grass was soggy. He had no energy. He laid his head on the cool saturated ground to rest and to wait for his strength to rebound. Squeezing the wet grass between his fingers, he dug out a wad and dragged it to his mouth. Even the mud tasted good. He sucked out the moisture, chewed on the gritty, soggy dead grass and then rested.

He wanted more. He told himself to get up and go to the corn crib. He tried to convince himself that it was only a short walk. He tried to tempt himself by imagining the taste of the corn kernel. Selu, corn, was the mother of man. She would save him. But his weak body would not respond. Dreams tried to push away his reason. Sweet dreams; so inviting. The world drifted away.

"Ugi?"

A distant voice calling his name from outside his head. His dream tried to incorporate it and make sense of it.

"Ugi?"

. . .

"Sakonige?"

THE RAVEN MOCKER IS A type of witch, whereas Stone Clad was a singular witch whose legend was told by the elders. Raven Mocker endured the ages and for some his kind still exists even today. The malicious witch that steals a man's souls was introduced to James Mooney by Cherokee elders and medicine men in the early 1800s.

James Mooney, author of voluminous works on the Cherokee including, "Myths of the Cherokee" and "Sacred Formulas of the Cherokee", studied the culture from 1887 to 1890 with the Bureau of American Ethnology.

"Mooney is recognized as the foremost student of Cherokee lore. His works remain the most comprehensive and authoritative to come from the pen of any scholar associated with the Bureau of Ethnology."

Following are excerpts from Mooney's manuscripts on "The Raven Mocker" and "Stone Clad". Recorded from extensive interviews with the elders, these are the stories that came down from the generations about these mythical men.

OF ALL THE CHEROKEE wizards or witches the most dreaded is the Raven Mocker (*Kâ'lanû Ahkyeli'ski*), the one that robs the dying man of life. They are of either sex and there is no sure way to know one, though they usually look withered and old, because they have added so many lives to their own.

At night, when some one is sick or dying in the settlement, the Raven Mocker goes to the place to take the life. He flies through the air in fiery shape, with arms outstretched like wings, and sparks trailing behind, and a rushing sound like the noise of a strong wind. Every little while as he flies, he makes a cry like the cry of a raven when it "dives" in the air—not like the common raven cry— and those who hear are afraid, because they know that some man's life will soon go out. When the Raven Mocker comes to the house he finds others of his kind waiting there, and unless there is a doctor on guard who knows how to drive them away they go inside, all invisible, and frighten and torment the sick man until they kill him. Sometimes to do this they even lift him from the bed and throw him on the floor, but his friends who are with him think he is only struggling for breath.

After the witches kill him, they take out his heart and eat it, and so add to their own lives as many days or years as they have taken from his. No one in the room can see them, and there is no scar where they take out the heart, but yet there is no heart left in the body. Only one who has the right medicine can recognize a Raven Mocker, and if such a man stays in the room with the sick person these witches are afraid to come in, and retreat as soon as they see him, because when one of them is recognized in his right shape he must die within seven days. There was once a man named Gûñskäli'skï, who had this medicine and used to hunt for Raven Mockers, and killed several. When the friends of a dying person know that there is no more hope they always try to have one of these medicine men stay in the house and watch the body until it is buried, because after burial the witches do not steal the heart.

The other witches are jealous of the Raven Mockers and afraid to come into the same house with one. Once a man who had the witch medicine was watching by a sick man and saw these other witches outside trying to get in. All at once they heard a Raven Mocker cry overhead and the others scattered "like a flock of pigeons when the hawk swoops." When at last a Raven Mocker dies these other witches sometimes take revenge by digging up the body and abusing it.

The following is told on the reservation as an actual happening:

A young man had been out on a hunting trip and was on his way home when night came on while he was still a long distance from the settlement. He knew of a house not far off the trail where an old man and his wife lived, so he turned in that direction to look for a place to sleep until morning. When he got to the house, there was nobody in it. He looked into the âsï and found no one there either. He thought maybe they had gone after water, and so stretched himself out in the farther corner to sleep. Very soon he heard a raven cry outside, and in a little while afterwards the old man came into the âsï and sat down by the fire without noticing the young man, who kept still in the dark corner. Soon there was another raven cry outside, and the old man said to himself, "Now my wife is coming," and sure enough in a little while the old woman came in and sat down by her husband. Then the young man knew they were Raven Mockers and he was frightened and kept very quiet.

Said the old man to his wife, "Well, what luck did you have?" "None," said the old woman, "there were too many doctors watching. What luck did you have?" "I got what I went for," said the old man. "There is no reason to fail, but you never have luck. Take this and cook it and let's have something to eat." She fixed the fire and then the young man smelled meat roasting and thought it smelled sweeter than any meat he had ever tasted. He peeped out from one eye, and it looked like a man's heart roasting on a stick.

Suddenly the old woman said to her husband, "Who is over in the corner?" "Nobody," said the old man. "Yes, there is," said the old woman, "I hear him snoring," and she stirred the fire until it blazed and lighted up the whole place, and there was the young man lying in the corner. He kept quiet and pretended to be asleep. The old man made a noise at the fire to wake him, but still he pretended to sleep. Then the old man came over and shook him, and he sat up and rubbed his eyes as if he had been asleep all the time.

Now it was near daylight and the old woman was out in the other house getting breakfast ready, but the hunter could hear her crying to herself. "Why is your wife crying?" he asked the old man. "Oh, she has lost some of her friends lately and feels lonesome," said her husband; but the young man knew that she was crying because he had heard them talking.

When they came out to breakfast, the old man put a bowl of corn mush before him and said, "This is all we have—we have had no meat for a long time." After breakfast the young man started on again, but when he had gone a little way, the old man ran after him with a fine piece of beadwork and gave it to him, saying, "Take this, and don't tell anybody what you heard last night, because my wife and I are always quarreling that way." The young man took the piece, but when he came to the first creek he threw it into the water and then went on to the settlement. There he told the whole story, and a party of warriors started back with him to kill the Raven Mockers. When they reached the place it was seven days after the first night. They found the old man and his wife lying dead in the house, so they set fire to it and burned it and the witches together.

Nûñ'yunu'wï
THE
STONE
MAN

Tʜɪs ɪs wʜᴀᴛ ᴛʜᴇ old men told me when I was a boy.

Once when all the people of the settlement were out in the mountains on a great hunt one man who had gone on ahead climbed to the top of a high ridge and found a large river on the other side. While he was looking across he saw an old man walking about on the opposite ridge, with a cane that seemed to be made of some bright, shining rock. The hunter watched and saw that every little while the old man would point his cane in a certain direction, then draw it back and smell the end of it. At last he pointed it in the direction of the hunting camp on the other side of the mountain, and this time when he drew back the staff he sniffed it several times as if it smelled very good, and then, he started along the ridge straight for the camp. He moved very slowly, with the help of the cane, until he reached the end of the ridge, when he threw the cane out into the air and it became a bridge of shining rock stretching across the river. After he had crossed over upon the bridge it became a cane again, and the old man picked it up and started over the mountain toward the camp.

The hunter was frightened, and felt sure that it meant mischief, so he hurried on down the mountain and took the shortest trail back to the camp to get there before the old man. When he got there and told his story the medicine-man said the old man was a wicked cannibal monster called Nûñ'yunu'wï, "Dressed in Stone," who lived in that part of the country, and was always going about the mountains looking for some hunter to kill and eat. It was very hard to escape from him, because his stick guided him like a dog, and it was nearly as hard to kill him, because his whole body was covered with a skin of solid rock. If he came he would kill and eat them all, and there was only one way to save themselves. He could not bear to look upon a menstrual woman, and if they could find seven menstrual women to stand in the path as he came along the sight would kill him.

So they asked among all the women, and found seven who were sick in that way, and with one of them it had just begun. By the order of the medicine-man they stripped themselves and stood along the path where the old man would come. Soon they heard Nûñ'yunu'wï coming through the woods, feeling his way with his stone cane. He came along the trail to where the first woman was standing, and as soon as he saw her he started and cried out: "*Yu!* my grandchild; you are in a very bad state!" He hurried past her, but in a moment he met the next woman, and cried out again: "*Yu!* my child; you are in a terrible way," and hurried past her, but now he was vomiting blood. He hurried on and met the third and the fourth and the fifth woman, but with each one that he saw his step grew weaker until when he came to the last one, with whom the sickness had just begun, the blood poured from his mouth and he fell down on the trail.

Then the medicine-man drove seven sourwood stakes through his body and pinned him to the ground, and when night came they piled great logs over him and set fire to them, and all the people gathered around to see. Nûñ'yunu'wï was a great ada'wehï and knew many secrets, and now as the fire came close to him he began to talk, and told them the medicine for all kinds of sickness. At midnight he began to sing, and sang the hunting songs for calling up the bear and the deer and all the animals of the woods and mountains. As the blaze grew hotter his voice sank low and lower, until at last when daylight came, the logs were a heap of white ashes and the voice was still.

Then the medicine-man told them to rake off the ashes, and where the body had lain they found only a large lump of red wâ'dï paint and a magic u'lûñsû'ti stone. He kept the stone for himself, and calling the people around him he painted them, on face and breast, with the red wâ'dï, and whatever each person prayed for while the painting was being done-whether for hunting success, for working skill, or for a long life-that gift was his.

The Sons of Raven Mocker

Book 2 of the Cherokee Chronicles Series

Courtney Miller

THE LEGEND OF THE Raven Mocker continues with the birth of his twin sons. Torn by the temptations of witchcraft and the influence of their mother and even their father to follow the white way, a struggle ensues that tears the family and the sons apart and creates a conflict that lasts a life time … and longer.

Here is an excerpt from the book:

Looking back, there is no time when I can definitely say that my brother ever showed compassion. Not even for himself. Maybe that is why I never understood his actions; why he always shocked me; why he scared me. I love my brother but I fear him more. I thought he loved me. Could he hate me so much if he did not once love me in equal measure? Isn't hate just love turned upside down? My wise friend Sali doesn't think so. He says that evil has no love component. Maybe he's right.

About the Author

Having retired after forty years in management, Courtney Miller has now embarked on the writing career he turned away from over four decades ago. Retirement has presented him with the opportunity to pursue the writing career he had been putting off all his life.

Combining into his writing his passion for archaeology, astronomy, archaeoastronomy and history, particularly that of the indigenous Native American cultures, Courtney here has set out to create a fiction series of books based on the Cherokee culture before and after the European invasion. The stories are brought to life through the hopes, struggles, triumphs, and challenges of his characters. Characters we would recognize and identify with today, but who lived in a very different society and a very different time.

To quote Courtney:

Grandmother believed she was one-quarter Cherokee, but I have tried to research our ancestors without much success. I did, however, discover that what I thought I knew about Native Americans was based on the Hollywood fixation on the Plains Indians. The Cherokee were nothing like these nomadic, hunter-gatherers. The Cherokee have been classified as one of the 'Civilized Tribes' for good reason. I want to begin to tell their story through the fictional eyes of a representative family living around 1000 a.d. and end the series with the tribe's relocation in the early 1800s.

After retiring, in 2012, Courtney and his wife, Lin, moved into the mountain house they spent eleven years building in the beautiful Wet Mountain Valley in southern Colorado. Inspired by the spectacular view of the Sangre de Cristo mountain range out his study window, Courtney is immersed in and loves his new life as writer and author.

In conjunction with his upcoming fiction book series, Courtney writes *Native American Antiquity*, a weekly blog focusing on Native American culture, presenting articles relating "how it was" to "how it is." The blog is published weekly, every Thursday.

You can follow Courtney on his website at:
www.CourtneyMillerAuthor.com

www.ingramcontent.com/pod-product-compliance
Lightning Source LLC
Chambersburg PA
CBHW021006120726
47905CB00009B/2874